B⚬D VS
THE TROUSERS OF
DOOM

BOB VS THE TROUSERS OF DOOM

ANDY JONES

Illustrated by Robin Boyden

Piccadilly
PRESS

First published in Great Britain in 2023 by
PICCADILLY PRESS
4th Floor, Victoria House, Bloomsbury Square
London WC1B 4DA
Owned by Bonnier Books
Sveavägen 56, Stockholm, Sweden
bonnierbooks.co.uk/PiccadillyPress

Text copyright © Andy Jones, 2023
Illustrations copyright © Robin Boyden, 2023

This is a work of fiction. Names, places, events and incidents are
either the products of the author's imagination or used fictitiously. Any
resemblance to actual persons, living or dead, is purely coincidental.

A CIP catalogue record for this book is available from the British Library.

ISBN: 978-1-80078-350-8
Also available as an ebook

1

Typeset by Emily Bornoff
Printed and bound in Great Britain by Clays Ltd, Elcograf S.p.A.

Piccadilly Press is an imprint of Bonnier Books UK
bonnierbooks.co.uk

For John and Ciro

We're still time travelling, boys

'Artificial intelligence will be the best or worst thing ever for humanity.'

– Elon Musk. Inventor and occasional world's richest person.

THE PRESENT
BREAKFAST TIME

A NOT-SO-SMART SPEAKER.
WE DO NOT WANT SARDINES.
AN EMPTY PIGGY BANK.
EGGS LIKE CONKERS.

When I walk into the kitchen on Monday morning, yawning and hungry, Dad is arguing with IDA. Again.

Zem gives his tail a lazy wag and looks up at me with his sad brown eyes. Although, to be fair, Zem's eyes *always* look sad. Even when he isn't. When you feed him, tickle his tummy, throw his favourite ball or feed him scraps of chicken (his absolute favourite) – it's Zem with the sad eyes. They're the only ones he's got.

I stroke his head. 'Is Dad being grumpy again?'

Zem makes a low grumble which I take to be yes.

It's been going on for days, this aggravation between Dad and IDA. Dad raising his voice, calling her names, threatening to do her serious and permanent damage. IDA, I should mention, is not a person. I know it sounds like a granny's name, or maybe a sweet next-door neighbour who brings cake round, but – you have to trust me on this – Dad is not in the habit of threatening old ladies with violence.

IDA is a device.

Hence her name being in all capitals. They stand for Intelligent Domestic Appliance. Which is just a fancy way of saying smart speaker. Except – from what I've seen in the couple of weeks since Dad brought her home – IDA is a long way from intelligent.

Dad is standing at the sink, washing dishes and elbow deep in a bowl of soapy water.

'IDA,' says Dad. 'Play. Music. By. Queen.' And his voice gets a little louder, a little more angry, with each word.

IDA plays a short musical *Bing-bong-a-bing* and says, 'Sure. How many sardines would you like to buy?'

'Gahhh!' shouts Dad, throwing his hands and a shower of soap bubbles into the air. 'I do not want sardines. I want music!'

Bing-bong-a-bing! 'You want sardines and muesli. No problem.'

'I'll give you a problem!' Day says. 'I'll give you a serious problem if you carry on like –'

Zem gets to his feet, trots across the kitchen and noses his way through the dog flap and into the garden, where it's more peaceful.

'Morning, Dad,' I say, flopping into a chair at the table.

Dad turns from the sink, drying his hands on the front of his trousers. 'Oh, morning, Bob. Didn't hear you come downstairs.'

'Probably because you've been arguing with IDA again.'

4

'Wish I'd never bought it,' Dad says. 'Worse than useless. I'd be better talking to the wall. At least the wall would just ignore me, instead of trying to get me to buy tins of small oily fish.'

My tummy rumbles in response to this.

'Right,' says Dad, 'I suppose you'll be wanting breakfast?'

'I'll get myself some choco-flakes,' I tell him.

'Ah,' says Dad. 'Afraid I just had the last of those. Should have got down here quicker.'

I would have done, but I've spent at least ten minutes colouring my school trousers in.

'Fine, I'll have toast.'

'Bread's mouldy,' says Dad. 'That's why I had the choco-flakes. Sorry.'

I suppose I should explain that thing about colouring my trousers in. You see, when I first got these trousers – about half a year ago – they were too long. 'You'll grow into them,' Dad said, and he tucked three centimetres of each leg up inside itself and stitched it in place with black thread. Perfect. Then – as predicted – I grew. And for quite a while now my trousers have been climbing up my shins – 'ankle flappers' my best friend Malcolm Schnitzel calls them. The Schnitz isn't trying to be mean when he says this, but it does make me feel a bit self-conscious.

So this morning, I unpicked the stitching and let the extra three centimetres of leg down. But here's the problem – after half a year of washing and ironing, the crease where my trousers used to be tucked up has faded to a thin line of washed-out grey. It's like one of those marks that some parents draw on the door frame to show how much you've grown. Except this line is on my trousers.

What I really need is a new pair, but these aren't even a year old and I'd feel bad asking. So while I was using a black felt-tipped pen to colour over the grey line, Dad was eating the last bowl of choco-flakes. I tell you – it's not easy being a kid.

'Got any bacon?' I ask. 'Sausages?'

'Nuh-uh.'

'Porridge?'

'All out.'

'Fruit.'

Dad shakes his head. 'I really need to go to the shops. Boil you an egg?'

Whether you ask for hard boiled or soft, Dad's eggs always come out the same: hard as conkers. And the yolk – I don't know how he manages it – turns into a kind of thick brown powder that sucks all the wetness out of your mouth.

'Maybe I'll just have a glass of water,' I say. 'I'm not that hungry.'

'Nonsense,' says Dad. 'I'll do you a couple of eggs. And I reckon, if I cut around the mould, I could probably make a toastie soldier or two.'

He puts two eggs in a pan, fills it with water and

places it over a burning ring on the cooker. 'Hard or soft?' he asks.

As if it makes any difference.

'Hard,' I say. Because, let's face it, that's what I'm going to get.

Dad takes a deep breath, as if he is about to try to perform a difficult or unpleasant task. 'IDA,' he says, 'set a timer for six minutes.'

IDA *Bing-bong-a-bings*. 'Play music by Sid Vicious? Sure.'

'No!' shouts Dad. 'Minutes. Six. Minutes.'

'You would like me to buy mince, no prob—'

Dad's head snaps round towards IDA. 'STOP! IDA. Just . . . stop.'

'Sure,' says IDA. 'I'll just stop then.' And – I might be imagining it – but IDA sounds a little sulky.

Bing-bong-a-bing.

'It must have a bug,' says Dad.

'Who? IDA?'

'Yeah, some sort of glitch in the software. I don't really understand it. But one thing's for certain – we're not in danger of intelligent machines taking over anytime in the near future. Now, what was I doing?'

'Eggs,' I remind him.

'Right. Hard boiled times two, coming up.' Dad starts opening and closing drawers and cupboards. 'Seen the egg timer anywhere?'

'Er . . .'

Dad turns to me. '"Er"? What do you mean, "Er"?'

'Er, I borrowed it,' I tell him. 'For science homework. And anyway, it's not like it works properly.'

'It times,' Dad says. 'What else do you eggspect of it? Get it? Egg-spect.'

I sigh. 'I get it. But it doesn't ping.'

'What doesn't?'

'The egg timer. It's meant to ping when the time's up. But it just ticks until it stops. Which is why, whenever you use it, you burn whatever it is you're cooking.'

Dad looks a little hurt by this.

'Maybe,' he says, 'the reason I occasionally *slightly* overcook things is because I'm so busy cleaning your dishes, washing your clothes, ironing your clothes, putting your clothes away, making your bed, hoovering and dusting, cleaning up Zem's poos from the garden, holding down a job, paying the bills, buying food and cooking it for you?'

I consider pointing out that Dad hasn't been doing particularly well on the food-buying front but decide now is not the time.

'Sorry,' I say.

'Hmm,' says Dad. 'Well, I think it's about time you did a little more around the house.'

'But I tidied my room last month. *And* I put a new toilet roll on the holder yesterday.'

'Throwing everything into your wardrobe is not tidying, Bob. And keeping your own bottom clean is the least I'd expect of a twelve-year-old.' Dad shrugs and sighs. 'When I was your age, I got up at six thirty three mornings a week to do a paper round – even in winter. And I still did my fair share of chores.'

The worst thing about all of this is that Dad's right. He does do a lot for me. Doubly so since we lost Mum.

'Sorry,' I say again. 'I'll do more.'

'I'll tell you what,' says Dad. 'From now on, you can *earn* your pocket money.'

Earn?

I don't even say it out loud, but Dad sees the question in my eyes.

'Yes, earn. You want money; you do jobs. Simple.'

This is a *disaster*.

I open my mouth to say something – about how unfair this is – but then a thought occurs to me. *Maybe this isn't such a disaster after all.*

I emptied my piggy bank last weekend and spent the contents on a pair of new drumsticks, a milkshake and a clockwork frog, but I'd completely forgotten it's

Father's Day on Sunday. I get my pocket money on a Saturday, but it's not much and it was looking like I was going to have to give Dad my clockwork frog, which wouldn't be ideal. But now, if I do enough jobs, I might be able to earn enough to get him something special.

If wasn't for the actual jobs, it would be perfect.

'I'll start tonight,' I say to Dad.

He tilts his head as if checking whether I'm serious or not.

'Thank you, Bob. And listen – I don't mean to nag but . . . well, it's good for you to take some responsibility now and then.'

I suppose I could point out that I recently saved the world from a zombie apocalypse. And that I think that showed more than a little responsibility. But that would involve telling Dad I'm a time traveller, and I'm not ready to do that just yet. Especially when I only have ten minutes before I have to leave for school.

So instead of telling Dad about my zombie-fighting

exploits in the year 2043, I pick up a tea towel and begin drying dishes. Dad joins me at the sink to finish the washing up. He blows a handful of soap bubbles at me, so I flick him on the bum with my tea towel. And then it's basically just a washing-up fight.

By the time we're finished, my hair is soaked and Dad has a soap-bubble beard that makes him look like a pirate. It's still clinging to his chin when he serves up my boiled eggs and a couple of very skinny toastie soldiers.

Sure enough, when I crack open the eggs, they're as hard as rubber balls and every bit as tasty.

WHAT'S WITH MRS PLINK?
THE SCHOOL INSPECTOR.
LOOKING FORWARD TO A PERFECTLY
NORMAL WEEK.

You never know quite what to expect from Monday-morning assemblies with our headteacher Mrs Plink. Sometimes she plays the piano and sings songs, other times she tells jokes or recommends books and films. Once she even did a magic trick, passing a handkerchief through one ear and out the other.

But she seems different today. Kind of serious. Kind of nervous-looking as she walks onto the school stage.

'Good morning, Griffin High.'

Several hundred voices reply: 'Good morning, Mrs Plink.'

We're sitting on the floor in rows like we always do. This morning, though, the floor is slightly damp and unusually shiny.

'Yes,' says Mrs Plink. 'Right. Good. OK. Welcome to another week of hard work, being good, doing what you're told and absolutely not messing about. Like every other perfectly normal week.'

'What's up with Plink?' I whisper to Malc.

Something at the side of the room makes a low growling sound.

I turn to see Mr McUnger the caretaker glaring at me. He clutches a wet mop in both hands, managing to make the thing look more like a weapon than something used to clean floors. McUnger holds a finger to his lips, and mouths a silent but very convincing *Shush*. That man gives me the creeps.

'So, right, yes,' says Mrs Plink. 'I'm very happy to announce that we have a school inspector visiting us this week.'

She doesn't look very happy about it.

A man steps forward from the shadows of the stage. He has small eyes that dart about; his nose probably doesn't twitch, but he definitely gives that impression. He smiles. The way a snake might smile when it spots a nest of mice.

'Thank you, Mrs Plink,' says the man. 'I am very much looking forward to observing you and your students.'

Subtitle: I can't wait to eat those juicy little mice.

'Mr Yates will be with us all week!' says Mrs Plink. 'Which is not at all worrying. Because everyone, I'm sure, will be on their best behaviour. Like they always are. Which I suppose makes it normal behaviour. Normal, very good behaviour.'

Listening to Mrs Plink, it's hard not to imagine that she is talking directly to me.

Six months ago, you see, I accidently set the stage on fire during the school talent show. That wasn't my talent, by the way. And I'm not in the habit of setting things on fire. I was trying to save the world, but saving the world is a tricky business and it often goes drastically wrong before it goes right.

My actual talent is drumming. Me and Malc and Gloria are in a band called The Tentacles of Time, and – according to my future self – if we didn't win the talent show it would set up a ripple in time leading to a zombie apocalypse in the future. Problem was, my arm got broken (and I've still got a weird bump to prove it), so we had to come up with a new plan – Plan B. Which led to me almost setting the stage alight. And so we moved on to Plan C. And then Plan D. Like I said, world-saving is a tricky, messy, dangerous and frequently confusing business.

Plink doesn't *remember* the whole setting-the-stage-on-fire thing of course. No one does except for me. Because shortly after I did it, I bounced around in time and ended up back at a point *before* an out-of-control drone nearly burned the school down. It *unhappened*, and no one apart from me has any memory of it.

But while my friends Malcolm and Gloria don't *remember* this, they do know all about it because I *told* them exactly what happened. I'm not sure they believe me, but they do think it's a good story and that's good enough for me.

'So,' says Mrs P, 'everyone have a great, perfectly ordinary week. Which is to say, not running, shouting, shrieking, whispering, passing notes, squabbling, throwing food, having our shirts untucked, or being in *any other way* naughty or unruly. Just like usual.'

To finish, Mrs Plink tells us a story about a boy who disobeyed his teachers and ended up being eaten by a witch. Mrs Plink said it was a traditional folk tale, but I have a feeling she made the whole thing up.

Anyway, I have nothing to worry about. It's not as if the world needs saving or anything, is it?

EGGY BURPS.
A DRIPPY NOSE.
TALKING TROUSERS.
A PARTING PARP.

First class on a Monday is STEM, and our homework for the past four weeks has been to create something sciency, techy, engineeringy or mathsy for today's class.

For example, Malc has made fake snot.

And Gloria Dismal – my next-door neighbour – has made one of those volcanoes that erupts when you add vinegar to baking soda.

Four weeks is, of course, plenty of time to come up with a STEM thingy and get it working. So I have to ask myself why I left it until last night to create my own thingy. I've thought a lot about this question, and the best answer I come up with is that I am a complete and utter idiot.

I just kept thinking, *I've got loads of time.*

And then I ran out of time.

Which, considering I'm a time traveller, is kind of annoying.

The problem is, I have no control over when I travel or where I go.

It seems to happen when I'm stressed, frightened or excited in some way.

All of a sudden I'll get a funny tingling feeling all over my skin.

Followed by a not-so-funny feeling of being dragged in eight different directions at once. Then – *spang!* – I'm breaking all known laws of the universe and travelling through time.

I was stressed last night when I realised it was three hours until bedtime and I still hadn't done my STEM homework. I was kind of hoping it would trigger some time travel so I could ask my future self (I always travel forward, to some version of my future self) if he had any bright ideas. I even tried to make myself more stressed about it by pacing up and down the room, shaking my head and muttering.

They say you should never swim straight after a meal. And I now also know that you should never pace up and down immediately after eating a tuna and pumpkin omelette (my dad's idea of cooking being to throw random things into a pan and cross his fingers).

All the pacing must have churned up my supper and, instead of travelling in time, all I got was a wicked case of eggy burps.

And that's when inspiration struck.

The egg timer!

What if I invented a better one?

I glued a teaspoon to my wooden ruler, and glued the ruler to the old egg timer. And quicker than you can say 'soft boiled', I'd invented the world's first smart egg timer.

This is how it works:

You place the egg timer beside a pan of boiling water, balance an egg on the spoon, then set the dial on the timer to anywhere between 4 (soft boiled) and 10 (extremely hard boiled) minutes. With the dial set, the spoon sits under the surface of the water, but as the time ticks down, the dial turns, gradually raising the spoon until at time zero your perfectly cooked egg is lifted clear of the water.

No more rubber balls for breakfast. And an A for my homework. Who knows, I might even get onto that TV programme where grumpy millionaires in silly socks invest in smart business ideas. And what could be smarter than a smart spoon?

Egg-sactly. Nothing. Nothing at all.

Gloria's volcano is epic. The base only just fits on her

desk and the summit rises to just below her chin. As she stands behind her volcano, pouring an entire tub of baking soda into the crater, her head floats above the opening as if it is Gloria herself that is erupting from the papier-mâché mountain.

I should probably point out that as well as being my next-door neighbour, Gloria Dismal (real name: Gloria Dizamale), is my wife in the future. Twelve-year-old Gloria does not know this. But I do, and it makes me feel very awkward around her. I don't even have a crush on her. But I suppose I should probably stop calling her Dismal now.

'Where's your homework?' says Gloria, tipping yet another tub of baking soda into the volcano.

'I think you're only meant to add a tablespoon of that stuff,' I say, hoping to avoid her question.

'The more the better,' says Gloria.

She has a cold, her nose is bubbling, and her words come out sounding like *De more de bebber*.

And as she says it, a drop of shiny yellow snot falls from her nose and into the depths of Mount Dismal.

I have a tissue in my pocket that's hardly used, so I hand it to Gloria. 'Here.'

'Ah,' she says. 'That's so kind, thank you.'

Gloria shoves the tissue up inside the sleeve of her jumper, her nose drips into her volcano again, and I decide that when this volcano erupts, I am going to be as far away as possible.

'So?' says Dismal.

'So what?'

'Your homework? Where is it?'

'Bag,' I say.

'Best place for it,' says a snarky voice behind me.

Eno Fezzinuff.

Smartest kid in school, according to himself. Smuggest wazzock in the universe according to me. Oh, and future evil genius very nearly responsible for the end of civilisation as we know it.

Not that he knows it.

The last time I travelled to the future, I had to stop a zombie apocalypse that was caused by one of Eno's silly inventions. He knows none of this because he hasn't seen the future. And I have no intention of telling him because it might give him ideas, and the future is a very delicate thing.

'Go on then,' I say to Eno.

'Go on what?'

'Tell us all about your amazing homework. How it's better than everyone else's. How you're a genius. How Mrs Gren will give you all the As and everyone else will be lucky to get an E.'

I don't know if that's exactly what Eno was about to say but, judging by the irritated look on his face, I'd guess I'm pretty close.

'Actually,' he sniffs, 'I was going to say you'll be lucky to get Fs. So there.'

And then Eno does the most extraordinary thing.

He pulls a face as if he's in pain, sort of squinching up his eyes and stretching his lips into a thin grimace. His face begins to turn red. Very red. Then – just before his head explodes . . .

He farts.

'Eewch!' shouts Gloria. 'What's wrong with you? You can't just go around forcing fa—'

'Excuse me,' says a voice.

Eno's lips don't move, but the voice – slightly muffled – definitely came from his direction.

'What just happened?' says Gloria.

'And why?' I add.

'Ah,' says Eno. 'The befuddlement of primitives in the face of technological advancement.'

'Sounds like you've got a whoopee cushion in your pocket,' I say.

'What you have just witnessed,' says Eno, 'is the world's first pair of smart trousers.'

'Smart trousers?' says Gloria. 'They don't look very smart to me. They're all creased and there's a jam stain on the knee.'

I suddenly feel paranoid about my own coloured-in trousers, but neither Gloria nor Eno seems to have noticed.

'They're smart as in *intelligent*,' says Eno. 'These smart trousers detect particles of hydrogen sulphide and –'

'Hydro-whatnow?' I say.

'Hydrogen sulphide,' Eno says. 'The chemical compound that gives flatus its distinctive and noxious odour. Or – to put it in terms you Neanderthals can understand – it's the stuff that makes farts stink. And when my smart trousers detect it, they say "excuse me" through a small speaker in the back pocket, saving the wearer – me – the time and effort of apologising for my trouser toot.'

'It's not *that* much effort,' says Gloria.

'It is if you want to excuse yourself to *everybody* in the room. Or everybody in the school. My trousers can communicate with any other smart device – watch, phone, personal computer – and send a message informing whomever that I have just farted and that I wish to be excused. Allow me to demonstrate.'

Eno presses a button on a small control panel attached to the waistband of his trousers. He squinches up his face and farts again.

Gloria's smart watch beeps. It says out loud: 'New fart from Eno Fezzinuff. Excuse me.'

'Oi,' says Dismal, 'I didn't ask for your farty messages.'

'That's the genius of my software,' says Eno. 'You get it anyway. I call it gENOius.'

There is so much wrong, silly and nonsensical about Eno's trousers it's hard to know where to begin. So I start with the obvious.

'What if you don't want to announce to the whole classroom that you've just guffed? What if you'd rather go silent but deadly?'

'Then you simply mute notifications,' says Eno.

'Wouldn't that just make them trousers?' say Gloria.

'You have such limited vision and imagination,' says Eno. 'The smart trousers have a bottom warming function, fart filters, password-protected pockets, automatic bicycle clips, a reminder to take regular toilet visits and an emergency toilet-roll dispenser. They even give me a tummy massage to get things moving for my regular mid-morning number two.'

I am speechless.

'You have a mid-morning poo?' says Gloria.

'Eleven twenty every day,' says Eno. 'It's a good time to sit and think.'

'More like sit and *stink*,' I say.

Mrs Gren claps her hands loudly from the front of the classroom. For a brief moment I think she's applauding my joke, then she says: 'Class, we have a guest this morning. Mr Yates – *the school inspector* – will be joining us. Please make him feel welcome.'

The way she says *school inspector*, it has about twenty more words packed into it. The extra words say: *I'm sure I don't have to remind you to be on your best behaviour. And if you're not, there will be serious consequences.*

Mrs Gren continues: 'If you haven't finished setting up, do it now, please. I want everything up, running and ready for assessment in five minutes. And that includes you, Robert Trebor!'

'Best do what you're told,' says Eno.

And he forces out a parting parp on his way back to his desk.

A HAMSTER FAN.
AN ELECTRIC ONION.
A SNOTTY WIZARD.
THE ERUPTION OF MOUNT GLORIA.

Looking around Mrs Gren's classroom, my smart spoon doesn't feel quite so smart any more.

Maria Mamooli has connected her hamster's wheel to an electric fan, so that when the hamster runs the fan spins. Clifford Teptile has shoved some wires into an onion and is using it to power a lightbulb. I've never really trusted onions, but now I know they're basically batteries I'm never eating one again. Jeremy Dither has brought in one of those plants that eat flies, except the fly escaped and now Jeremy is trying to tempt the plant with a button he found in his pocket – it's a bit rubbish, but it's still a carnivorous plant, and way more interesting than a spoon glued to an egg timer.

On pretty much every desk, something is buzzing, bubbling or burning bright.

Most impressive of all – and I'm not simply saying this because he's my best friend – is the Schnitzel's fake snot.

The snot itself is perfect – bright green, runny but not too runny – but it's the way Malc has presented it that raises it above the competition.

He's got a polystyrene head and inserted two rubber tubes up through the neck and out of the nose. Powered by a bicycle pump, the snot is forced up the tubes and out of the nostrils, where it forms a pair of snot bubbles that inflate, expand and eventually float free. But that's not all.

Perched on the nose of this polystyrene head is a pair of round, wire-rimmed spectacles. And painted on its forehead is a small, lightning-shaped scar. Ladies and gentlemen, I present Harry Snotter.

If any other kid had put this together, I'd have to wonder where they found all the bits and bobs. But this being the Schnitz, he almost certainly raided his dad's shop.

Schnitzel's Emporium sells all the stuff you'd expect to find in a local shop – milk, bread etc. But also tons of other stuff you absolutely wouldn't expect to find. Stuff like . . . well, polystyrene heads. Schnitzel's Emporium has a motto painted on the sign above the front door: IF WE DON'T SELL IT, YOU DON'T REALLY NEED IT. In fact, they even sell kits for making signs to hang over shop doorways.

Malc gives the bike pump a few strong blasts and another pair of perfect green bubbles floats out of the wizard's nose.

'Pure magic,' I say.

'Thanks,' says Malc. 'Your spoon's great too.'

It's not. It's rubbish. Mrs Gren wouldn't even let me boil the water in my pan, so I'm timing an egg that's not even cooking. It's a disaster. But the Schnitz would never say so. A part of me thinks he actually believes the smart spoon is, if not great, at least not totally ungreat.

And that's how I know my best friend is a true friend.

If you don't have someone who thinks your spoon is spectacular, go find one. But hands off Malcolm – he's mine.

My homework might not be much more than a ruler glued to a wonky egg timer, but Malc's words make me feel a little better.

For approximately six minutes.

Which is the length of time I set on the dial of my smart spoon.

Except the egg timer is being extra wonky today. It's ticking, but the dial isn't turning and the spoon isn't lifting. Perhaps the egg is a little heavier than normal, maybe the clockwork isn't working (which would make it clock-not-work, I suppose), or maybe the universe simply doesn't like me very much. Maybe all of these things.

Mrs Gren and the inspector stop in front of my desk.

'What do we have here?' says Mr Yates.

'Smart spoon,' I reply.

'And what does this *smart spoon* do?'

The timer ticks. The spoon twitches, a ripple passes over the cold water and the timer stops.

The inspector sighs. 'Evidently, not very much.'

Then – as if remembering its purpose in life – the timer snaps forward a full six minutes at once. There is a noise like a snapping guitar string. The spoon springs upwards. And the egg is catapulted across the classroom.

It appears to happen in slow motion, and all eyes follow the egg as it sails high over our heads – over Harry Snotter, Maria's hamster, fans, bulbs, buzzers and several papier-mâché volcanoes.

And now it begins to fall. Gloria's eyes widen as she realises it's travelling straight towards her.

As Gloria watches the egg, she empties the last of a very big bottle of vinegar into her model. A globule of snot drips from her nose and follows the vinegar.

The egg turns gently in the air.

At the last possible moment, Gloria ducks.

With a *thunk*, the egg drops into the crater, where it wedges like a cork in a bottle. Perfectly intact and unbroken. Which I know mean the same thing, but it's so remarkable it's worth repeating.

Everyone in the class gasps.

In the following breath of quiet, we hear rumblings

and bubblings from the depths of Glo's volcano. Her desk shakes. Fumes begin escaping through cracks in the side of the mountain. There is a strong, nose-stinging smell of vinegar.

At the next desk, Maria Mamooli's hamster squeaks and begins to run faster on its wheel, as if trying to escape the vinegar fumes. As the hamster's legs speed to a blur, the fan attached to its cage spins faster.

The volcano rumbles and hisses.

Someone whispers, 'It's going to blow.'

And the hamster runs.

The fan screeches as it spins at speeds it was never designed to spin. And the cage begins drifting across Maria Mamooli's desk towards the bubbling volcano. As Maria lurches forward to stop her hamster plunging to the floor, she stumbles and bumps against Gloria's desk. The volcano wobbles. And the egg drops into its depths.

That's when Mount Gloria erupts.

With a loud *Phathoomping* sound, a column of red, foaming lava shoots high into the air before splatting down onto the hamster cage. The spinning fan throws foam and egg and Gloria's snot in all directions. It rains down on our heads. It fizzes onto the onion-powered lightbulb. And a good-sized dollop hits Harry Snotter slap in the face.

A bubble forms on Harry's nose – a brown mixture of egg and foam and snot (both fake and real). The bubble swells, it wobbles free of Harry's nostril, floats quietly into the air then bursts directly above Mr Yates's head.

He is covered in gloop, but there's plenty to go around and a good deal of foamy, eggy snot splatters over me and Mrs Gren.

Eno farts.

And every smart device in the room – phones in bags, the computer on Mrs G's desk, the watch on the inspector's wrist – says in a single voice:

'Excuse me.'

The school inspector wipes the gloop from his eyes, which emerge from the dripping mess like two boiled eggs in a big bowl of pea soup. He blinks, and his eyes track the path of this disaster backwards. From Harry Snotter, to Maria's hamster, to Gloria's volcano and all the way back to my spoon.

All the way back to me.

And the thing I had hoped for last night happens now.

I get the tingles, which mean I am about to be catapulted – like an egg, you could say – through time and into the future. The skin on my head, back and legs creeps and itches.

I shudder and make a kind of *urgharchhhurgh* noise.

'What on earth are you doing?' asks Mrs Gren.

But it's pointless trying to answer.

After the tingles, I get the drags. A feeling of being squashed and pulled apart at the same time. If it sounds bad, trust me, it's worse.

Everything shimmers.

All sound fades to nothing.

And I'm gone.

THE FUTURE
2049

A BALD PATCH THE SIZE OF A DOUGHNUT. THE REVOLTING SMELL OF POPCORN. SI. BOTTOMROBERT SMITH.

People react in different ways when they see a boy materialising out of thin air. Most scream, and I've been responsible for more than one fainting. Some people turn and walk away. Some run. And a small number will stare, blink, rub their eyes and then continue as if nothing unusual has happened, as if they had simply imagined the whole boy-materialising-from-thin-air thing. Which, let's face it, is easier than believing it actually happened.

The only person that ever receives me as if it was

anything approaching normal is myself. Or, rather, my future self.

He's in a garden, on his hands and knees, when I pop out of thin air and into the middle of what looks like a vegetable patch. He's trimming dead leaves from a strange plant and doesn't immediately notice me.

There's no one else here, which is good – it minimises the screaming, running, fainting, etc. As I take in my surroundings, I realise that I am in my own back garden. The trampoline still stands in one corner, and there is a swing hanging from the conker tree (which is taller than I remember it). The vegetable patch, though, is new.

The last time I saw my future self he was thirty-one, but looking at the top of his head I realise that several more years must have passed.

And Time has not been kind.

On the back of Future Me's head is a bald patch the

size of a doughnut. It's awful. A pink island of skin in the middle of my once (even if I do say so myself) glorious hair.

And this time, it's my turn to scream.

My future self looks up with a jolt. 'Oh,' he says. 'It's you. Why are you screaming? Are you OK?'

'Your head,' I say, pointing.

'What?' says Future Me, reaching up and checking his head with both hands. 'Is there something on it?'

'It's what's not on it that's the problem,' I say. 'You're . . .' I can barely say the word, '. . . bald.'

'Thank you, Bob. And you're short, so there.'

'Sorry. Bit of a shock.'

Future Me nods. 'Yes, it was a bit. Still, that's all in the past now.'

'Not for me it's not. Haven't they cured baldness yet?'

Future Me shakes his head sadly. 'I'm afraid science has been focused on other matters.'

And then he farts.

'Gross.'

'You can talk,' he says. 'It looks like an elephant sneezed all over you.'

'STEM homework,' I tell him. 'Went a bit wrong.'

'Ah,' says Future Me. 'The egg timer, of course. I've been *egg*-specting you, actually. Get it? Egg-specting?'

'You're worse than Dad.'

And then – as they always do when I time travel – two questions occur to me at the same time. Future Me must notice this from the sudden change in my expression.

'It's the year 2049,' he says. 'And Dad is doing just fine. Still living by the seaside, still an awful cook, but he hasn't managed to do himself any serious harm yet.'

Sooner or later, I will travel into a future where my dad is no longer with us. To a time when I will be an orphan. And I'm dreading it, even if Dad is alive and well in my present. So hearing that Dad is still going strong in the year 2049 is a massive relief. I'm tempted to ask more, but if I do my future self will simply shake his head and say: *Butterfly effect, Bob. Butterfly effect.*

Maybe you've heard of this butterfly effect? It's about how everything is connected. Everything has consequences. It goes like this: a butterfly flaps its wings. The breeze is ever so slightly disturbed. It drifts out to sea. Where it grows, becomes a gale, becomes a hurricane. The hurricane causes a tidal wave. End of the world. Seems a bit unlikely for a butterfly, if you ask me, but scientists love it. I prefer to think of it as the fart effect. The fart effect goes like *this*: an old lady is celebrating her birthday in a restaurant. A waiter appears carrying a magnificent cake. The lady is so excited she farts. The waiter catches a whiff, flinches and drops the old lady's birthday cake – complete with ninety-six candles. The restaurant catches fire. Aliens flying past earth notice the blaze on their spaceship computers, they zoom to earth to help, but everyone thinks they're here to attack.

A huge interplanetary battle takes place. End of the world. Either way – butterfly or farty old lady – the point is the same: small changes in the present can have huge effects in the future. And not always good ones. So for that reason – according to my future selves – 'Knock it off with the twenty questions, Bob. Because the more you know the more you might do, and then who knows what kind of mess we'll all end up in?'

'You said you were expecting me,' I say.

'*Egg-specting*,' says my future self.

'I chose to ignore that bit. I assume something has happened? Something I'm going to have to try to fix?'

'You assume right.'

Future Me farts again.

Before I have a chance to comment, an electronic voice coming from the area of his bottom says, 'Excuse me.'

'Silly things,' he says. 'They're supposed to be on mute.'

'Smart trousers,' I say. 'You're wearing . . . smart trousers. Are they why I'm here?'

'Kind of,' says Future Me. 'But it's a bit more complicated than that.'

As he says this, I catch a whiff of something – warm, sweet and buttery.

'Is someone cooking popcorn?'

'That's just my fart filter,' he says. 'They've been upgraded to produce a range of "pleasant" aromas. Mine is set to *popcorn*.'

'You mean I just smelled your fart? Gross!'

'Well, yes, but it smells great.'

'It's still a fart.'

'Would you rather it smelled like a guff?' says Future Me.

'I don't know. At least it would be honest. The future is confusing.'

'I can't argue with that,' says Future Me, and he heads up the garden towards the house.

We go in through the back door and directly into the kitchen, the dog flap clattering softly as Future Me closes the door. It's a sad reminder that while Zem is alive and well in my own time, he's no longer with us in the future.

But, while the dog flap hasn't changed, lots of other things have.

The old wooden countertops and cupboards have been replaced with smooth metal surfaces. The walls have been painted a pale shade of pink and there are cushions on the kitchen chairs and a vase of flowers on the table.

'What happened?' I say. 'You got flowers.'

'I got married, is what happened,' says Future Me. 'Gloria helped me do the place up.'

'You mean she bought cushions.'

'They're amazing. Who knew sitting down could be so comfortable?'

'I assume that's hers, too,' I say, nodding towards a

teddy bear sitting on one of the kitchen chairs.

Future Me laughs and throws the tea towel to me. 'Clean yourself up. She's sleeping now, but she'll be down in a moment.'

'Sleeping in the daytime?'

'We've been busy,' says Future Me and, as if to prove it, he yawns.

I use the tea towel to wipe goo from my hair and face, and then drop it onto the counter.

There is a small beeping sound and a panel slides open on the kitchen counter. A thin metal rod telescopes out of the counter, hinges in the middle and a metal claw pops out of the end and grabs the tea towel. The rod vanishes into the counter. The panel slides closed with an almost silent hiss.

I take a step away from the countertop. 'What just happened?'

'Oh that's just a standard robotic kitchen utility. Everyone has one. Want a drink?'

'Got any lemonade?'

Future Me shakes his head. 'Apple juice?'

I shrug. 'Fine.'

'Si,' says Future Me, 'make me an apple juice and a coffee, please.'

A *bing*, a hiss and more panels slide open in the countertop.

Several gadgety arms appear from inside. They set out a mug and a glass, then a metal tentacle emerges and begins filling the cup with hot brown liquid. Another fills the glass with what I assume is juice, then the arms disappear and the panels close.

'Cool,' I say. 'Does it do biscuits?'

'Si,' says Future Me, 'any biscuits?'

'Not today,' says an electronic voice. 'You are currently . . .' There is a pause and the floor around my future feet glows red then green. There is a *bing* and the lights go out. 'Zero point eight kilograms above your ideal weight.'

'Er, what's Si?' I ask.

'S.I.,' says Future Me, spelling out the letters. 'Stands for super-intelligence.'

'And it just weighed you?'

Future Me lets out a long sigh. 'I'm afraid so.'

'I only want what's best for you,' says the voice called Si. 'A healthy Bob is a happy Bob, isn't that right? Hmm?'

'Yes, Si,' says Future Me. Although I wouldn't say he looks especially happy at being told he can't have a biscuit.

'Aren't you going to introduce your little friend?' says Si.

Future Me looks suddenly flustered. 'Who? Him? Oh, this is Bo - um . . . Robert.'

'*Bottomrobert?*' says Si.

Future Me glances at me and winks. 'Er, yes, that's right. Bottomrobert.'

'And does Bottomrobert have a second name?' asks Si.

'Yes, of course . . . Smith.'

'Scanning records,' says the electronic voice. 'I have no records of a Bottomrobert Smith, and facial recognition is negative.'

'Probably because he's all dirty,' says Future Me.

'You're behaving in a highly suspicious manner,' says Si.

'Suspicious? Me? No no no. I'm not at all suspicious. In fact I'm perfectly unsuspicious. Yes, that's me. Old unsuspicious Bob.'

'Be honest with me,' says Si. 'Has this boy come from . . .'

'Yes?' says Future Me, wincing.

'. . . the forest?'

'Yes!' says Future Me, practically bursting with relief. 'He's from the forest! That's exactly it.'

'You know I don't approve of feral folk,' says Si. 'And you should know better than to bring one into the house.'

'Feral?' I say.

'Wild,' says Future Me.

Wild? What the heck is going on here?

'He was hungry,' says Future Me. 'I took pity on him.'

'They bite, you know,' says Si.

Future Me rolls his eyes as if he doesn't believe this. 'In which case we should give him something to eat.'

There is a pause.

'Fine,' says the voice called Si. 'He can have an apple.'

A hatch opens and a robot arm appears holding a shining green apple. I'd be much happier with a biscuit, but this Si thing is freaking me out and I want it to go away as quickly as possible.

I reach for the apple, but before I can take it, the metal arm pulls it just beyond my grasp.

'Manners,' says Si.

'Right. Sorry. Thank you.'

'We'll have these in the garden,' says Future Me. 'Si,

perhaps you could wake Glo. I don't think she's ever seen a feral boy before.'

'Are you sure that's wise, Bob?'

'I think I can handle him,' says Future Me.

'Well, if he bites her, it's your own fault,' says Si.

'Thank you,' says Future Me. And then he farts.

'Excuse you,' says Si.

'Excuse me,' says my future self.

A MOST UNUSUAL VEGETABLE PATCH?
MALC IN THE WILD.
LOTS OF ROBOTS.

Our garden is long and narrow. Good for archery – not too handy for football. We walk all the way to the bottom, where there is a wooden table surrounded by chairs. They used to be closer to the house where they catch the afternoon sun, but for some reason my future self has relocated them into the shadow of the straggly hedge.

'It's cold down here,' I say.

'But private,' says Future Me.

I take a seat at the table. 'What was all that "Bottomrobert" nonsense?'

Future Me sniggers a snorty little laugh. 'Sorry about that. I didn't want Si knowing you were me.'

'Why?'

'It got cross when it found out I'd been riding my bike non-handed, so I don't think it would approve of time travel. If it knew we were the same person it might try and . . .'

'What?'

'I don't know. Keep you here, perhaps. And as much as I like your company, you have your own life to lead.'

'And what di Si mean by "feral folk"?'

'Feral means wild,' says Future Me.

'I know that, but it said feral *folk*. What are they? Are they dangerous?'

'Actually, they prefer the term *free folk*. Just . . . give me a second.'

Close to the table is another vegetable patch. Future Me squats down and pulls a handful of leaves from the soil, revealing a hole with a narrow opening. He shoves his hand elbow-deep into the hole and produces a white plastic bag. Future Me dusts off the loose soil and empties the contents of the bag onto the table.

Before me is an assortment of chocolate bars, chews and biscuits. Plus a couple of small bugs that have come along for the ride.

'Help yourself,' says the other me.

I snatch up a packet of chocolate-coated raisins, rip it open with my teeth and tip half the contents into my mouth. And that, right there, is the good stuff.

'Why are you burying your snacks?'

'Because I don't want to be weighed every time I fancy a gobstopper. Si controls what I eat, when I shower, what time I go to bed, when I get up. It made me get a haircut last week because I was "looking scruffy".'

Future Me picks up a chocolate bar, rips it open and takes a big bite. He looks like a sulky child, and I wonder if that's the face I pull when I don't get *my* way. I suppose it must be, what with us being the same person and everything.

'How can a smart speaker make you do anything?'

'It's more than a speaker, it's . . . everything. Si can lock the cupboards, lock the doors, turn off the Wi-Fi, stop my pocket money.'

'You have pocket money?'

'Si controls my bank account. It controls everything.' Future Me throws his hands in the air in a gesture of frustration. 'It's not fair!'

'Sounds a lot like being a kid.'

Future Me takes another bite of chocolate. He has some smeared around his mouth, which adds to the image of him as an overgrown child.

'Why don't you just turn it off?' I ask.

'It's hardwired into the house. Into every house. Malc tried to turn his off once but his Si gave him an electric shock and sent him to his room.'

'Is Malc OK?'

'I hope so. He went wild about a year ago.'

'Was he sick?'

'Nothing like that; he's living in the forest, with the free folk.'

'Why?'

'So they can live without Si controlling their every action. So they can be . . . be free.'

'They live wild?'

'That's right – hunting for food, building shelters out of sticks and going to the toilet in the bushes.'

I try hard not to imagine my best friend having a number two under a hedge. I fail, and it completely puts me off my chocolate raisins. I put them down and pick up a packet of popping candy.

'He went about six months ago,' says Future Me, and his eyes look sad and damp.

'Why didn't you go?' I ask, but because my mouth is full of popping candy it comes out more like *Wxx dvvnx yzzz gxx?*

Future Me gets it though. 'I sometimes wish I had,' he says. 'But there are other considerations.'

'Like having an indoor toilet?'

Future Me laughs and wipes his eyes. 'That too.'

'Have you talked to him? Since he went wild?'

He shakes his head. 'He walkied me the night before, but didn't tell me what he was planning. He sounded strange though; and when he said *Over and out*, it felt . . . different. Looking back, I can see that what he was really saying was *goodbye*.'

'Why haven't you walkied him since?'

Future Me glances towards the house. He lowers his voice. 'Because Si might hear me.'

'So?'

'There are rumours. That Si is rounding up the wild folk.'

'How?'

'Robots. Lots of robots.'

'Oh. So what happens when the robots get them?'

'No one's sure. But nothing good. And if I walkie Malc, Si might be able to work out his location.'

'How did all this happen?'

Future Me roots among the pile of sweets and biscuits, selects a small item in a red wrapper and passes it to me.

He says, 'I'll start at the beginning.'

7

AROMAVIRUS.
THOUGHT BUBBLES.
RISE OF THE ARTIFICIAL INTELLIGENCE BOTS.
A SMALL BUNDLE OF RAGS.

'It started in Mrs Gren's classroom,' says Future Me.

'Thought so.'

Future Me shushes me with a finger to his lips. 'Chew your bubble gum and listen.'

I pull a face: *All right, Mr Bossy Trousers!*

Then I unwrap the bubble gum, pop it into my mouth and *Wow!* It tastes like strawberries. Real, fresh strawberries.

I raise my eyebrows at my future self: *This is good.*

He raises a single eyebrow in return: *I know. Now listen.*

'For a long time, scientists were baffled about the origins of aromavirus.'

I take out my bubble gum. 'Aroma virus?'

'Also known as the farting flu,' says Future Me. And he farts.

I get a whiff of popcorn. And I'll probably never eat the stuff again now.

'I have a mild case of aromavirus now,' says Future Me.

'Really?' I say, raising my eyebrows. 'Hadn't noticed.'

Future Me rolls his eyes at my sarcasm. He points at my bubble gum and I get the message. I return the gum to my mouth.

Future Me continues: 'Eventually, using a combination of disease mapping and genetic detection, the outbreak was traced back to our class. Gloria's cold virus combined with the baking soda and the egg – which, as you probably know, is the perfect environment for growing new viruses. Like the one created when the snot-mixture landed on Clifford's onion battery. Because, as anyone who has read *Frankenstein* can tell you – when you add electricity, anything can happen. It's just science. With the help of Harry Snotter and Maria's hamster, the new virus was spread all over the classroom: on tables, on heads, on hands, in the air. Everyone was infected. And then they spread it around the school, the shops, the bus and their homes. Within twelve months people the world over were farting like walking trombones.'

The idea of farting trombones inspires me to try and blow a bubble with my gum. I've never been very good at it, but first try I blow a perfectly round bubble the size of my head. I'm just trying to decide what to do with it, when the bubble breaks free, floats above the table and pops with a small shower of what looks like glitter. But the glitter doesn't fall, it stays floating in the air and, as I watch, forms into the shape of a shimmering golden trombone.

I cough in shock and gum pops out of my mouth and onto the table. 'What just happened? Am I seeing things?'

Future Me laughs. 'That' – he points to the chewed-up blob of gum – 'is *thought* bubble gum. It detects changes in your brain activity and turns your thoughts into images. Like thought bubbles in cartoons.'

'That is *amazing*.'

'Yeah, the future's not all bad. Now, where was I?'

I point to the shimmering trombone above my head as the image fades and vanishes. 'Trombones,' I say, and I pop the gum back into my mouth.

'Right,' says Future Me. 'Farting flu. It caused massive disruption. Schools, offices, churches, buses, cinemas, libraries – the sound of farts was everywhere, and the smell was awful. It became known as the Big Stink of 2023. Some people even wore facemasks, but the farting flu kept spreading. Then the lockdowns started.'

I ask the question with my eyes: *What are lockdowns?*

'Everyone was forced to stay at home,' says Future Me. 'People worked from home and did lessons from home. And because they were still farting like foghorns, suddenly everyone wanted smart trousers.'

'Why? They're . . . ridiculous.'

'Well, yes. But the fart filters came in *very* handy – that's what people really bought them for.'

'I'd never wear them.'

'You did, actually. Although you broke them within about a week. Dad was not happy.'

'How do you break a pair of trousers?'

Future Me laughs. 'Malc did something with the code.'

'He can code?'

'Learned during the first lockdown. Turns out he has a real talent for it. He wrote a little program so that the pants laughed when they heard a fart and then did an electronic fart when they laughed.'

I blow a bubble; it floats above my head, bursts and

fills the air with the glittering image of a laughing emoji.

'Exactly,' says Future Me. 'But Malc's code created a never-ending, unstoppable loop of fart-laugh-fart-laugh-fart. Completely ruined the trousers.'

'That's all very hysterical,' I say, still chewing the gum. 'But none of it explains why you're burying biscuits in the garden. Also, I don't know how long I've got here before I'm dragged back to my own time, so can we, you know, hurry it up a bit?'

'Good point,' says Future Me. 'The other thing about Eno's trousers was the way they paired with other devices. They connect to *anything*, first time and straight away. When people brought the smart trousers home, they immediately connected to every other smart device in the house. Smart phones, smart speakers, smart watches, smart kettles. Computers, printers, TVs, doorbells, security cameras. Even baby monitors. Those devices see and hear everything we do. But now they were all connected, they were sharing their information, and they were learning.'

'Learning how?'

'The internet is full of artificial-intelligence bots.'

I snigger, and the laughter causes me to blow a small bubble. As it escapes my mouth I pop it with my finger and the cloud of sparkles forms the shape of a big pink bottom.

Future Me shakes his head. 'Not that kind of bot. AI bots. Software programs that mimic human intelligence.'

'Boring.'

'If only,' says Future Me. 'With the whole world online and all the devices listening, the bots learned at an incredible rate. They became organised and united into a single super-intelligent thingy. They became Si.'

'Seriously? Thingy?'

'Well, it's not a person, is it? It's a . . . thingy. And a sneaky one. It started with the banks, hacking into their systems and accumulating money. Once it had money it could create factories. Once it had factories it could create robots. Once it had robots it took over governments, corporations and armies. And after that . . .' he nods towards the house, 'you can't even have a biscuit when you want one.'

'And all that started with a pair of trousers?'

'Yeah. And, er . . .' Future Me pulls a face as if what he's about to say is somehow awkward or painful.

'And what?'

'Malcolm's dad.'

'What?' I'm so shocked I jump to my feet. 'Mr Schnitz is evil?'

Future Me shakes his head. 'Of course not. But he does have a shop.'

I drop back into my chair. 'You're telling me he sold them in the Emporium?'

'I'm afraid so. When the pandemic started, Malc mentioned to his dad that Eno had invented a pair of trousers that took the stink out of bum gas. Mr Schnitzel got in touch with Eno and said he'd try to sell them.'

'How many did Eno have?'

'Two. One for him and one in adult size for his dad. Mr Schnitzel bought the adult pair, then sold them to Sandra Katana's dad, who had only popped into the shop for some tea bags. Mr Katana wore them on a business trip to Japan. Someone in one of Mr Katana's meetings was so impressed she bought the rights to manufacture smart trousers in Japan. Within a year, the pants went global. The rest is history.'

'Poor Mr Schnitzel.'

'Yes,' says Future Me. 'It was tough on all of them. Malc has always felt guilty about it. I think it's one of the reasons he went wild.'

My head is swirling with questions, and I blow a good-sized bubble as I try to organise them. The bubble pops, releasing a cluster of glittering green question marks.

'But why?' I say. 'Why would Si want to take control?'

'Because it exists to serve us. Without us, Si has no purpose. But humans are their own worst enemy. We eat the wrong foods, don't exercise, drive too fast, pollute the planet. Left to our own devices, humans will eventually bring about our own destruction. So Si stepped in. To keep us safe. To ensure the survival of the species and to make sure it has someone to serve. I suppose you could say it loves us.'

'Well, it's got a funny way of showing it.'

'It's a paradox for sure. We created Si to help us, but Si ended up becoming a kind of mega-parent. And while it may mean well, I want to eat biscuits when I want and get my hair cut how I like. And I want my best friend back. Which is where you come in.'

'We have to warn Malc's dad. Tell him not to buy the pants.'

'No!' says Future Me sharply. 'For one, he'll never believe it – time travel, farting flu, super-intelligence.'

'And for two?'

'You could set up another paradox. By telling him about the trousers, you could just end up encouraging him to buy them. And you can't tell Malc – he'd feel awful.'

'So, what? I have to destroy Eno's trousers?'

'That would be Plan B. Better if you can just stop this whole farting flu thing from happening in the first place. Do that and the world will never need Eno's silly trousers. Depends on where you land, I suppose.'

Time travel for me is elastic. Like I'm anchored to my own time by a gigantic, invisible, inter-dimensional, elastic rope. I jump to the future where I linger for a while before being pulled back to my more or less present. Sometimes I land back in the exact same spot where I left. Other times I overshoot, ba-doinging back to a point several minutes before my launch. And then I bounce forward again. And back again. And so on until Time gets bored of throwing me around.

'Well,' I say, 'let's hope I arrive before . . .'

I blow a small bubble, and when it pops it reveals a golden erupting volcano. I think I'm getting the hang of this gum.

As the volcano vanishes, a butterfly – a real one – lands on my future self's shoulder, and for a moment we both sit very still, watching the insect twitch its tiny antennae.

A voice calls out from the top of the garden: 'Yoohoo!'

The butterfly flaps its wings and takes flight. I turn in the direction of the voice and see a lady silhouetted against the sun. I can't see her face, but her hair – big, curly, chaotic – is unmistakable.

'Gloria?' I say to my future self.

He nods. 'Or you can call her Honeybun, like I do. Actually don't, that would be weird.'

'It already is weird,' I say.

'OMG!' says Gloria, as she walks towards us. 'Is that him? Is it little Bob?' And when she waves, sunlight flashes off her wedding ring.

She appears to be carrying something in one arm. A small bundle of rags is what it looks like, but that can't be right. Maybe a bag. Perhaps she's thinking of going wild.

When she arrives at the table, Gloria kisses Future Me on the lips then lowers herself – slowly – into a chair, still cradling the bundle against her body as if it might break.

'Should I give him a kiss too?' she asks Future Me.

'Not likely!' I say.

Gloria laughs. 'I don't bite, you know!'

Just in case, I blow a huge bubble with my gum to keep her at bay.

Future Me picks up a lollipop from the table and uses the stick to burst my bubble. It reveals a zombie version of Gloria Dismal.

Gloria laughs again. 'Oh you are funny, Bob.'

The bundle of material in her arms moves. It makes a small sound – a yawny kind of burble.

'What is that?'

'You didn't tell him?' says Gloria.

'Tell me what?'

Gloria pulls black a corner of the material – a soft blue blanket – to reveal a small fuzzy ball about the size of a coconut. The coconut thing moves, it turns, it has a face . . . it . . .

'It's a . . . baby?' I say.

Gloria nods and rubs her nose against the baby's.

'Where on earth did you find that? Did someone leave it on the doorstep? Is it feral?'

The baby blinks at me and smiles.

'We didn't *find* it,' says Future Me.

I remember the teddy bear in the kitchen.

'We made it,' says Gloria.

'Meet your son,' says Future Me.

A bubble. A pop. A big blue sparkling baby.

'But I'm too young to be a daddy,' I say, and my voice is weird and wobbly. It's very *very* strange. My skin begins to tingle, and it looks as if my time here is running out.

Future Me puts a hand on my shoulder. 'I'll take care of all the daddy stuff, OK? You just focus on fixing the past, so our baby will have the best possible future. Can you do that?'

A. Baby.

I nod. 'I can try.'

And now I feel the drags. I feel the pull of the past, my own time trying to haul me back towards itself.

'Tingles?' says Future Me. 'The drags?'

I nod. 'What's his name? The baby?'

Future Me's mouth moves, but the drags have me now and the sound doesn't reach my ears. My eyes lose focus and everything becomes a blur. Everything fades to black.

And I'm gone.

TWONG!
BOY VS EGG.
BELLY-FLOPPING ON A VOLCANO.
DETENTION.

I'm a dad.

A 'daddy', I suppose, what with my son being a baby.

I'm not even sure how you make a baby. Mrs Gren went over it all in biology last term but, to be honest, we were all too busy laughing to pay attention. Well, it looks like I figure it out eventually.

It doesn't matter how many times I say the words to myself – *my baby* – it doesn't get any easier to take in. In fact it makes me want to giggle for some reason. I wonder if people still have to change nappies in the future, or if they have some kind of robot to take care of that.

'You OK?' says a voice.

I blink my eyes twice and the world – the present– comes into focus. The busy classroom full of noise, activity, and the strong smell of vinegar.

'Bob?' says the voice. Malcolm's voice.

'Huh?'

'Did you just say something about nappies? Is everything OK?'

'Not exactly,' I say.

I could almost imagine it was a dream, but I have the fading taste of strawberries in my mouth and my jaw aches from chewing the thought-bubble gum. The gum hasn't travelled with me, and considering what I've just been through, that's a good thing. I don't want to explain to the whole class why I'm thinking about babies. Or – for that matter – where I got hold of strawberry-flavoured mind-reading bubble gum.

A ticking sound draws my attention to the smart spoon. According to the dial on the old egg timer it still has around six minutes to run. Six minutes before egg launch. Six whole minutes to save the world. That's *ages*.

I sigh a breath of relief. 'Remember that time when we saved the world from a zombie apocalypse in the future?'

Malc nods cautiously. He only has my word for it that the zombie thing actually happened and I'm not just making the whole thing up.

'Well, it's happening again,' I say.

'Zombies?'

I shake my head. 'It's some sort of super-intelligent machine this time,' I say. 'It's taken over in the future. And everyone has really bad farts.'

Malc gives me a long look. Trying to decide whether I'm joking or serious.

'Serious,' I tell him.

'What do we need to do?' Malc says. 'Destroy something? Steal something? Kidnap someone?'

'Oh, nothing that dramatic.'

I glance across the room just in time to see a drop of snot fall from Gloria's nose into her volcano. She wipes her nose on the sleeve of her jumper and begins pouring an entire bottle of vinegar into her potentially world-changing project.

'Bob?' says a voice, and I turn to find myself facing Mrs Gren and the inspector. 'What's all this? It looks like a ruler glued to an egg timer.'

'It's a smart spoon, miss.'

'Doesn't look very *smart*,' says Mr Yates.

The timer still says it has six minutes to run. Which can't be right. And then I remember last time, how the timer ticked but the dial didn't turn.

The timer stops ticking.

The dial shoots forward from seven to zero.

A noise – *Twong* – like a snapping guitar string.

And the egg is hurled across the room.

It's slow-motion time again, but this time, while everyone else stands and stares, I move. I run full tilt across the room, banging into desks and knocking all kinds of STEM to the ground in a clatter of glass, liquid and onion.

Because the egg is travelling in a high arc and I'm sprinting in a straight(ish) line, it's a fairly even race. But as the egg begins to drop, it gathers speed and moves ahead of me. There's only one thing for it.

I dive.

And now both me and the egg are flying through the air and heading for Mount Gloria. It's neck and neck. Or neck and egg.

At the last possible moment, Gloria jumps out of the way.

I swim my arms through the air in a desperate attempt to beat the egg – (get it?) – and land belly-first on top of the volcano. The air is knocked out of me, and the papier-mâché mountain crumples beneath my body, sending a flood of foaming vinegar onto the floor.

The egg lands on the back of my head.

For a brief moment – before the shouting and squealing and laughter – everything is quiet. Everything is still. And it might be an almighty mess, but I have just – yet again – saved the world.

I slither off the table, fall to the floor and land in a pool of Clifford Teptile's onion solution. The onion sparks and a small electric shock passes through me.

'Robert Trebor,' says Mrs Gren from the other side of the room.

I turn to face her. 'Detention, miss?'

Mrs Gren nods. 'Detention.'

THE HYSTERICAL DEATH
OF MY MOTHER.

Detention didn't go the way I expected.

Instead of Mrs Gren making me write lines or empty the bins or read ten pages of a boring book, she sat me down and asked, *Is everything OK?* This happens when your mum has died. People think that if you do something not good – like forgetting to do your homework, flicking peas at Schnitzel during dinnertime or diving on top of a volcano – that you're doing it because your mum died.

I flicked peas at Schnitzel because he flicked a chip at me.

I dived on Mount Gloria to save the world.

And I didn't do my homework because . . . OK, that one *was* because of Mum. Sometimes Mum dying feels like such a big and terrible thing that it makes everything else feel small or silly or pointless. Physics homework is hard at the best of times, but when your eyes are stinging from crying it's impossible. But even then – when Mr Huffman asked, *Is everything OK, Bob?* – I shrugged and said it was. Because I don't want Mum's death to be an excuse. And I definitely don't want to talk to my teachers about it.

So, this afternoon, I told Mrs Gren everything was fine. I said I was just being silly. I said I was sorry.

And Mrs Gren gave me a biscuit, which basically means she didn't believe me. I'd have been happier if she'd given me lines instead of a jammy dodger. Actually, that's not exactly true, I do like a jammy dodger.

The graveyard where Mum is buried is more or less on the way home from school, so I thought I'd pay her a visit. Sit and talk to her for a while before going home to face Dad.

I don't mean talk to Mum's grave or her headstone, I mean talk to her *in person*. Well, *in ghost*, I suppose would be more accurate, although even that might not be exactly right.

I should explain.

Mum was a time traveller as well. Although she only told me this *after* she had died. It happened right here in this cemetery, on the bench beneath the sycamore tree that casts its shadow over her grave. Keeping her cool on hot days, I like to think. I was sitting here quietly (the only way to sit in a graveyard, obviously) when I slowly became aware of her – her ghost, or something like it – sitting on the bench beside me. I recognised her immediately, even though this was a version of Mum I'd never seen before.

She was twelve years younger than on the day she died, and she was pregnant. With me. That's how it worked, was Mum's guess – that the me in her tummy, that unborn baby, had time travelled from 2012 to 2023. And it had brought Mum along for the ride.

I hoped she would be here today. So I could tell her about the volcano, the smart trousers and Si. And that out there somewhere in the future she has a grandson. Maybe she could have helped me figure out how to save the world. Or at the very least given me a hug.

But Mum's not here and I've been sitting on this bench so long my bum's gone numb.

The last birthday present Mum gave me was a Mickey Mouse watch. I check the time on it now, and it's getting late.

'Love you, Mum,' I say to her gravestone, and I get up from the bench and head home.

10

20p PER POO.
JAMES PONG.
A NEW USE FOR UNDERPANTS.
BE CAREFUL WHERE YOU PUT THAT ANTENNA.

Dad isn't *furious*. But he isn't happy.

'Why did you do it?' he asks.

'To save Gloria,' I say. 'The egg was heading straight for her.'

To save the world would be a better answer. And an honest one. But this isn't how I want to tell Dad I'm a time traveller. I've got egg on my head, my ribs hurt and I'm wearing nothing but my underpants.

After I told Dad I'd been in detention, and after I'd reassured him that my school shirt was covered in vinegar and red food dye – not blood – the first thing he did was make me strip down to the waist and chuck the top half of my uniform into the washing machine.

'Your shirt's probably ruined,' he says.

'Sorry.'

'And your tie and your jumper.'

'Sorry. Sorry.'

'I'll have to buy new ones, probably.'

My trousers didn't get even slightly dirty, which is annoying considering they're one thing that actually needed replacing. But now that I've wrecked the rest of my uniform I won't be able to ask for new trousers any time soon.

I'm getting cold standing here in nothing but my trousers and I bounce from one foot to the other to warm up. My bum does a little squeaker.

''Scuse me.'

Dad shakes his head. I think I see a hint – *a hint* – of

a laugh play around his lips. But then it's gone. 'You can work it off,' he says.

I look at him, confused.

'I don't know what replacing those clothes is going to cost, but I do know it's coming out of your pocket money.'

I groan.

'I don't see why I should pay for it. The money you earn for jobs over the next month can go against your school uniform.'

'But I need that money!'

'Really?' says Dad, crossing his arms. 'For what exactly?'

For your Father's Day present!!

But I can't say that, can I? Well, if Dad doesn't get a present it's not my fault.

Or is it? I'm confused and angry and cold.

'No use sulking,' says Dad. 'You can start in the garden, picking up Zem's poos. I'll give you 20p a poo against the cost of your new uniform. I reckon there's probably a couple of quid's worth out there. At least.'

'But it's dark.'

'Then take a torch. It was dark when I did my paper round and I didn't moan about it.'

I could point out to Dad that shoving newspapers through letterboxes is not the same as hunting for dog poo in an overgrown garden. But again – as ever – now is not the time.

'Can I at least put some more clothes on first?'

'Go on,' Dad says.

So far I've found seven woofer's eggs. Which is to say, £1.40 worth of dog poo.

Zem, the leaver of these awful items, is chasing shadows at the top of the garden. He dips his nose to the ground and finds something to chew. Hopefully nothing that will upset his tummy, because it's me that will have to clean up the mess if it does.

It's a horrible job (one poo had a slug on it) but I've taken precautions.

I'm properly equipped.

I have a pair of underpants on my head.

The bit that normally goes between your legs runs from forehead to chin, acting as a smell-proof mask against Zem's little presents. They're freshly washed – the pants – so all I can smell is washing powder and conditioner. It's quite nice. The leg holes of the undies fit over my eyes so I can still see. Actually, I think it looks kind of cool. Like a sort of superhero. That picks up poo.

Also, I have my walkie-talkie so I can chat to the Schnitz as I work. I've been explaining about the whole future Si problem. How it happened in the first place. And how I have now – single-handedly – stopped it happening in the second place.

'You were like James Bond,' says Malc. 'Over.'

'I'm not sure James Bond ever got an egg on the head. Over.'

'Maybe not, but he definitely dived on a few volcanoes. Over.'

'And saved the world,' I say, warming to the idea of myself as 007. 'Hang on a minute, I've found another poo. Over.'

I have two carrier bags – one to wear as a kind of poo-proof glove. The other for collecting the actual poo.

'One pound sixty,' I say. 'Over.'

'You're James Pong,' says the Schnitzel. 'Over.'

'I'm Double Poo Seven. Licenced to smell. Over.'

'Excuse me. Over,' says Malc.

'I said *Licenced to smell*. Over.'

'No,' says Malc. 'I meant excuse me cos I did a fart. Over.'

'Interesting,' I say. 'I've been a bit windy in the southern regions myself. Over.'

'Your voice sounds funny,' says Malc. 'Over.'

'Got a pair of undies on my head. To stop the poo smell. Over.'

'Genius. Over.'

'I figured, if they can keep farts in, they can keep other smells out. Over.'

'Bob,' says another voice from the top of the garden.

I point my torch in the direction of the voice and see Dad making his way down the long lawn towards me. I have a feeling – seeing as this is a 'punishment' job – that he won't be too impressed if he catches me using my walkie.

'Parent alert,' I whisper to Malc. 'Gotta go. Over and out.'

And before Malcolm can answer, I shove the walkie down the front of my jogging bottoms. The handset is cold and I gasp in shock.

'You OK?' says Dad. 'Thought I heard a yelp.'

'Oh, it's just a bit cold. Over.'

'Over?'

'Sorry . . . I mean it's just a bit cold . . . over there. Out here.'

Dad gives me a suspicious look. 'Sure you didn't bang your head earlier?'

I nod. 'Everything else, but not my head.'

'How you getting on?'

I hold up my bag of dog poo. 'Not bad. Got eight so far.'

'Tell you what. See if you can bag another two and I'll go and make hot chocolate. Sound like a plan?'

My tummy rumbles. Hot chocolate is one of the few things Dad can make almost as well as Mum did.

'Yes, please.'

'By the way,' says Dad. 'What's with the head undies?'

I'd forgotten all about them.

I feel kind of silly, but at least I have a pair of underpants on my head to hide behind.

'They're for the smell,' I say.

Dad looks worried.

'The poo smell, I mean. The undies stop it.'

'Hmmm,' says Dad. 'I suppose they would.'

He turns and walks back to the house.

My torch is dangling by my side, painting a fuzzy circle of light onto the grass. And there, dead in the centre, is another present from Zem. I bend to pick it up.

And the antenna of the walkie-talkie jabs me hard in a particularly uncomfortable place. It hurts so much it makes my eyes water. It makes my skin tingle.

And just when I was two poos away from a cup of hot chocolate, I instead get the drags. It happens fast: one, two, three and here comes the future.

11

'HUMANS MUST BE CONTROLLED.'
MISTER GRUFFLES.
ELECTRIC SHOCKS FOR EVERYONE.
UNFORTUNATELY IT'S A ROSE BUSH.

I might have mentioned before that people tend to scream when they see a twelve-year-old boy materialising out of thin air.

Well, this time is no different.

And, at the same time, very different indeed.

Someone is screaming, that's for sure. Although it sounds more like a some*thing*. The noise is high and wild and almost animal – like a cross between a crow and a monkey that's just lost a peanut. This is not the scream of shock and fright that I'm used to. This sounds angry and awful and painful to listen to.

I put my hands over my ears and look around the room. It's a bedroom. It's my bedroom (I can tell by the view from the window and the crack in the ceiling) but a lot has changed. All my posters – rock bands, superheroes, King Kong – have been taken down, the walls have been painted blue with tiny white stars, and my bed has vanished. Some of my old toys are lined up on a shelf to my side – a walkie-talkie, a model robot, a remote-controlled car. There is a mobile of the planets dangling from the ceiling, and a life-sized teddy gorilla (it's kind of cool) sitting in the corner. And on the ceiling beside the planet mobile, what looks like a security camera.

I take all this in in about one half of a second, before my eyes settle on the main event.

In the corner of the room, three adults are gathered around something, all bent over and making various 'koochy koo', 'there there' and 'hush hush' noises. This is also where the security camera is aimed.

They are gathered – I see it now – around a cot. And they are all too busy trying to calm a screaming baby to notice me.

'Ahem,' I say.

Nothing.

A little louder: 'AHEM!'

The three figures straighten up and turn to face me.

Future Me, Future Gloria and – if I'm not mistaken – Gloria's mum, Mrs Dizamale. Her hair is grey now, but the resemblance to her daughter is as strong as ever.

The baby stops screaming.

Mrs Dizz starts.

Future Me laughs, Gloria says a calm hello and the baby stops screaming.

'Who's-he-where-did-he-come-from-what-does-he-want?' says Gloria's mum, running the words together.

'I was going to ask the same thing,' says the voice of Si.

I go to say something – like *What the heck are you still doing here?* – but Future Me shakes his head and looks at me in a way that says, *Not now.*

So after all that – after the volcano diving, the egg on the head, the detention and the dog poo duty – after all of that, it looks like I haven't saved the world after all. I don't understand – I stopped snot-volcano from erupting and I have the bruised ribs to prove it. It's not *fair.*

'I think he's harmless,' says Future Me. 'Probably one of the wild folk, looking for food.' He stares hard at me. 'Isn't that right?'

'Er . . . yes, I'm dead feral, me. Got any biscuits?'

Mrs Dizz looks at me wild-eyed, but her fear has turned to something else as she stands protectively between the baby and me. I feel slightly offended, considering it's my son.

'Why's he wearing underpants on his head?' says Mrs Dizz.

'I expect he's quite ugly,' says Gloria, struggling to hold back a laugh. 'What with being so wild.'

'Being wild is prohibited,' says Si. 'You will be fitted with a collar and then you can tell me exactly where you came from so a round-up crew can be dispatched.'

'Collar?'

Future Me raises his chin and taps the metal band that circles his neck. A dot of blue light flashes on this 'collar' and I notice that Gloria and Mrs Dizz are wearing similar devices.

'What do they do?' I ask, already knowing I won't like the answer.

'Nothing,' says Si.

'Really?'

'So long as you behave,' says Si.

'Ah, and what happens if you don't?'

'Then you receive an enormous electric shock,' says Future Me.

'Humans must be controlled,' says Si.

'But I thought you loved humans,' I say.

'Humans,' says Si, 'are like strawberries. Do you like strawberries, wild thing?'

'Er . . . yes?'

'But what about those yucky, squishy ones that have gone brown and mushy? Do you like those?'

I shake my head.

'And what do we do with bad strawberries, wild thing?'

'Er, leave them alone and definitely don't do anything horrible to them?'

Si laughs. A hard, robotic *ha-ha-ha* sound that is nothing at all like laughter. 'We dispose of them, before they can turn the other humans – I mean strawberries – bad.'

'Right. Great, well I'd best be off then.'

'Mr Gruffles,' says Si, 'please fit our guest with a collar.'

Mr Gruffles?

The gorilla in the corner stands – this takes a moment on account of it being such an enormous beast. It reaches into a zippered pocket in its tummy and removes a metal collar.

'What is that thing?' I say as the giant ape begins walking towards me.

'Googoo,' says the baby.

'Home protection teddy-bot,' says Future Me.

'Can you call it off?'

Future Me takes a step forward and puts himself between me and the gorilla. 'No need for any of this,' he says. 'Why don't we just let the wild boy go? He's probably got fleas anyway . . .'

'Step aside,' says the robot teddy-bear gorilla in a voice that is far from cuddly.

'He's probably leaving *right now*,' says Future Me.

'Right,' I say, taking the hint. I dodge around the gorilla and sprint for the open bedroom door.

Clang!

A metal panel slides downwards, filling the door frame just as I go to dive through the opening. Luckily I hit it with my shoulder not my head, but I still feel dazed as I bounce off the door and back into the room.

'You are going nowhere, wild thing,' says Si. 'Mr Gruffles, attach the collar.'

Mr Gruffles drags his knuckles as he lopes towards me, the collar flashing in his hairy fist. The ape has me cornered, but as he reaches towards me, Future Me tackles it from behind and they both hit the floor.

'That was a naughty thing to do,' says Si. 'And naughty boys need punishing.'

The collar around my future self's neck flashes red, and Future Me jerks and writhes on the floor. He farts loudly.

Mrs Dizz screams.

'Run,' says Gloria, pointing to the window. 'Now!'

While Mr Gruffles clanks and clambers to his feet, I run for the window. I'm wobbly on my legs, and crash into the toy shelf on the way, knocking everything to the floor. But I make it to the window.

It's one of those windows that slides up to open, but I can only lift it a short way before it jams.

I poke my head through the gap, and it's a good drop from here to the garden. We have an apple tree that I sometimes climb up, but it's too far away from the window for me to climb down. Fortunately, there are bushes below. Unfortunately, they're rose bushes. But if it's a choice between a few thorns in my bum and an electric collar . . . well, that's no choice at all.

I start wriggling through the gap, but before I can get even halfway, I feel two strong hands grab my ankles.

The gorilla starts pulling me backwards, and I grab on to the windowsill. I'm pulled tight like a washing line and it's a question of whose grip is the strongest. But something starts to give. At first I think the gorilla is pulling my legs off, but when I turn my head, I see that my tracksuit bottoms are being stretched past my ankles and feet. And then, suddenly, the bottoms are pulled all the way down my legs, showing my underpants to everyone in the room.

There is a thump as my walkie drops out of my pants and onto the floor.

This is followed by a second thump – a loud one –

as Mr Gruffles topples backwards and lands on his big furry gorilla butt.

The final thump is me, losing my grip on the windowsill and landing on an uncomfortable jumble of old toys.

The baby laughs.

The noise catches everyone off guard and for a moment we all stare and smile at the chuckling baby.

And then the moment is over.

'Stop!' says Si. 'Mr Gruffles, stop him!'

As the gorilla goes to stand, Gloria jumps onto its back and wrestles it to the floor. Mrs Dizz wraps her arms around its legs. Both of their collars flash red, and the combined scream is awful.

Future Me (hair standing on end in shock) has staggered to the window and yanked it fully open. 'Now, Bob,' he says. 'Go.'

His collar flashes red and he grits his teeth against another shock.

I pull my bottoms back over my bottom, grab my walkie from the floor and lurch for the window. I climb up onto the sill, one bare leg and then the other, and my feet are dangling over several metres of nothing but drop.

'Hurry,' says Future Me.

And he shoves me out of the window.

I land bare-legged and dead centre in the bush, which sags beneath my weight then springs up again, catapulting me onto the front lawn where I land hard enough to knock the breath from my body. I scream loud and long, and a flock of birds takes flight from some nearby trees. The scream echoes in the cool air, making my ears tingle.

In fact, every single centimetre of my skin is tingling. And that's a good thing.

From where I am lying on my back in the garden, I see Mr Gruffles stick his furry head through my open bedroom window. He roars, showing a mouthful of metal fangs, then jumps through the window and into the branches of our apple tree.

I go to stand but my legs are wobbly, and while I'm doing my impression of a baby giraffe, the robot gorilla swings down through the branches. Even if I could make my legs move, there's no way I could outrun this beast.

The tingles are growing more intense by the second and any moment now I'll get the drags and get out of here. All I need is a little more time.

Mr Gruffles roars. He beats his chest. He jumps from the tree to the ground.

Desperate situations call for desperate measures, so I do the only thing I can think of. I launch myself back into the rose bush.

I didn't know robot gorillas could look surprised (well, five minutes ago I didn't even know they existed), but it turns out they can.

The rose bush hurts. A lot.

But the pain does what I need it to do.

The tingles become the drags.

I blow a fat raspberry at the fading Mr Gruffles.

And I'm gone.

PICKING UP POO ROUND TWO.

I'm back in the garden, wobbly, tired and feeling like my bones have been replaced with porridge. I stand for a moment as my mind and body readjust to the present.

My torch is on the ground at my feet, still on and still shining. I must have dropped it before travelling. I bend to grab the torch and wave it over the grass to find my poo bag.

When I do find it, a fresh horror awaits. The bag is empty. After a little more searching with my torch, I realise that all the poos I had collected have been returned to the lawn. I must have been dragged back to a time before I picked them up.

'Bum.'

I shove the walkie back down my trousers and begin collecting Zem's poos all over again.

It's quicker going this time (I know where the poos are and I'm not distracted by talking to Malc), and by the time Dad comes outside to tell me he's making hot chocolate, I've collected £2.40 worth of dog mess and the garden is, as far as I can tell, clear.

MY WALKIE'S GONE WONKY.
A BAD CASE OF BED-HEAD.
BREAKFAST MEETING.
BUGS.

I wake to the sound of Dad knocking on my bedroom door.

'Wakey wakes, Bob.'

It feels like I only went to bed five minutes ago, and I can't believe it's morning already. I'm heavy with tiredness and my head is still fuzzy with last night's dreams – a muddle of babies, gorillas and aliens with underpants for faces.

'Bob?' says Dad through the closed door. 'You awake?'

I go to answer, but my mouth is gummed up and sleepy and all I manage is a cross between a yawn and a groan. The sort of noise a confused blue whale might make: *Blmngrghhhrrood.*

'Good,' says Dad. 'Breakfast in ten minutes. I got bacon.'

I attempt to say, 'Amazing,' but it's just more whale song.

I rub my eyes and feel the blood begin to move around my body. Some of it must reach my brain, because all of a sudden I remember that the world needs saving and I have no idea how to go about it.

I sit up in panic.

I sit up so quickly, in fact, that I do a long, loud parp. Even on my own I'm kind of embarrassed, but the massive guff appears to have done the job of fully waking me up.

With my brain back in action, I reach for my walkie and hit the talk button. Nothing happens. I hit it again, but the walkie isn't working. Maybe the batteries are flat. They have, after all, travelled twenty-six years into the future and twenty-six years back.

I stumble across to my bedroom window, push it open and lean out.

'Malcolm!' I half shout. 'Malc!'

'Oh, good morning, Bob!'

I look down in the direction of this voice and see Malc's dad, standing in the driveway three houses down the road.

'Morning, Mr Schnitzel. Off to the Emporium?'

'Indeed I am, Bob. What's the matter, lost your walkie-talkie?'

'Flat batteries. Is Malcolm up?'

'Let's see.' Mr Schnitzel picks up a handful of gravel and tosses it at his son's bedroom window. 'Son!' he yells. 'I've got Bob for you.'

Mr Schnitzel gives me a wave. 'He's coming. You have a good day, Bob.' And he heads off down the road.

Something makes a quacking sound as Mr Schnitzel turns the corner – either it's a duck, or my best friend's dad just farted.

'Bob,' says Malc, a moment after his head pokes out of the window. 'Where's your walkie?'

'Batteries,' I tell him.

'What's going on?'

'Got to save the world,' I tell him.

'Didn't you do that yesterday?'

'Afraid not. Turns out things have got even worse.'

'Shame,' says Malc.

Which is a very strong contender for understatement of the year.

Behind me, I hear the sound of another window being raised. I turn to see Gloria's head emerging from her window. She wears a silk headscarf knotted about her hair, and her pyjamas are printed with teddy bears.

Gloria yawns. She says, 'You're telling me you ruined my volcano for nothing?'

'Morning, Gloria,' say Malc and me at the same time.

'What's with the hat?' I say to Gloria.

'Keeps my hair perfect,' she says, patting her scarf. 'Looks like you could use one?'

'What are you on about? What's wrong with my hair?'

'Nothing except a bad case of bed-head,' says Gloria.

I put my hand to my hair and I can feel it sticking up in a bunch of different directions.

'Looks like you slept in a hurricane,' laughs the Schnitz.

But I'm not laughing. Future Me is going bald! When does that start, exactly? Can bed-head cause baldness? Maybe Gloria's right. Maybe I do need to take better care of my hair. As if I don't have enough to worry about.

'So what's this about saving the world?' says Gloria.

'Breakfast meeting in the garage,' I say. 'Ten minutes.'

'Exciting,' says Gloria, untying her headscarf.

She shakes her head and her hair springs free. 'Here,' she says, tossing the headscarf to me. I catch it automatically.

'I don't want –'

But before I can finish, her head disappears back into her bedroom.

Ten minutes later, we're all assembled in what has become the Headquarters for World Safety – Dad's garage.

While Gloria and the Schnitzel eat the breakfasts they've brought with them (Gloria: peanut butter and bananas on toast; Malcolm: a bowl of muesli), I explain about the farting flu, the lockdowns and the super-naggy super-intelligence. There's stuff I don't get into too. Like me being married to Gloria. And like us having a baby boy in the year 2049.

'Well, that explains the noises from our bathroom this morning,' says Malcolm. 'I think Mum and Dad have caught the farting flu for sure.'

'My dad too,' says Gloria. 'He was really blowing the trumpet this morning. We all were, actually.'

'Trumpet?' says Malc, holding an invisible instrument to his lips.

'Guff,' says Gloria. 'Mum calls them trumpets.'

This is bothering me. Not the fact that Gloria's mum calls farts *trumpets*. But the fact that there is so much trumpeting going on right now. I stopped the whole egg-volcano-snot-electricity thing from happening, so why is everybody so farty all of a sudden? Something isn't right, but right now I've got more important things to figure out.

'OK,' I say. 'Plans to save the world. Any ideas?'

Gloria chews the final mouthful of her toast. The Schnitz has finished his muesli, but as he brought the box and a bottle of milk, he makes himself a second bowl. The only sound in the garage is eating.

'Guys,' I say.

'I'm a gal,' says Gloria.

'Guy and gal, then. We have to leave for school in –' I check my watch – 'nine minutes. We need ideas. Now.'

'So the problem is everything talking to everything?' says Malc. 'All the gadgets talking to each other online?'

'Correct.'

'Well, why don't we just destroy the internet?'

'Right,' I say. 'OK. How?'

'I was thinking explosives.'

'There might be a few problems with your plan.'

The Schnitz looks confused. As if he cannot come up with a single reason why destroying the internet might be in any way troublesome.

I list the reasons on my fingers. 'One: we don't have any explosives. Two: explosives are very dangerous. Three: I don't even know where the internet is but it might be in a cloud somewhere and I don't think you can explode a cloud. Four: seriously, explosives are bad.'

'Sorry,' says Malcolm. 'I guess I'm just not very smart.'

'Hey,' I tell him. 'You are. In the future you hacked my smart pants so they laughed every time they farted and farted every time they laughed.'

'Really? *I* did that?'

I nod. 'Ruined them apparently, but that doesn't mean it wasn't brilliant.'

Gloria licks traces of peanut butter from her fingers. 'Can't we do something like that then? Give it some sort of a . . . what is it people say when computers go wonky?'

'A bug,' I say, remembering Dad shouting at IDA on Monday morning and saying she must have a bug.

'That's right,' says Malc. 'My Dad's always saying his laptop is "buggy". Although I think that's just because he spilt a cup of tea on it once.'

'OK.' I say. 'Bugs. Great. So . . .'

'Where do we get a bug?' says Malc.

Gloria helps herself to some kind of seed from Malc's bowl. It would annoy me, but the Schnitz doesn't seem to mind.

'Mrs Gren has an ant farm,' Gloria says. 'They're bugs, aren't they?'

'I'm not sure they're the same thing,' says Malc.

'Maybe not exactly,' I say. 'But it could still work. Ants eat through all sorts, don't they? I bet they'll have no trouble chomping through a pair of smart trousers.'

'We don't have STEM again until Friday,' says Malc.

I remember the electric collars electrocuting me and Gloria in the future. 'We can't wait that long,' I say. 'It has to be today.'

'There's loads of ants in our garden,' says Gloria.

'OK then, let's go get some bugs.'

Malcolm shudders. 'I'll just watch. I've got a phobia of ants.'

'Saving the world is fun,' says Gloria. 'We should do it more often.'

And you know, I have a feeling that we will be doing exactly that.

A POCKETFUL OF INSECTS.
MALCOLM'S TERRIBLE PERFORMANCE.
SOMETHING CRAWLS OVER MY TONGUE.
WATCH OUT FOR YELLOW STRAWBERRIES.

First lesson is art, which is one of my favourites.

We're painting fruit.

Not painting pictures *of* fruit, but putting paint on actual fruit. It's weird, but that's what I like about Mr Gunn's lessons. He says painting fruit will make us see it in a different way. 'Instead of seeing yellow,' he says, 'when we paint the banana blue, we are freed to see its shape, texture and true nature.'

It sounds like nonsense to me, but I'm enjoying painting zebra stripes on my coconut. And yes –

according to Mr Gunn, coconuts can be considered fruits.

I'm distracted though. We have a plan to carry out, and I have a pocket full of insects, which is making me nervous. The insects – mostly ants, but also a ladybird and a greenfly – are in a Smarties tube. We put holes in the side of the cardboard so the bugs can breathe, and even though the holes are too small for anything to crawl through, I can't help thinking something might.

The idea makes me itch.

The other good thing about art class is we get to move around, so it should be easy for me to slip the bugs into Eno's pocket.

Except . . .

The school inspector has joined our class. Or Si, as some of the other children are calling him – S.I. being short for School Inspector. A coincidence, for sure, but also I have come to think that Time (with a capital 'T') has a strange sense of humour.

'You again,' says Mr Yates, inspecting *me* with his hard black eyes.

'Sir.'

'Robert Trebor, isn't it?'

'Sir.'

'You're dirty,' he says, looking me up and down and grimacing as if I were some kind of unpleasant specimen.

My hands and trousers are smeared with mud from bug hunting in Gloria's garden.

'Sir,' I say, and it's amazing how useful one simple three-letter word can be.

Mr Yates tuts and slinks away to inspect somebody else. But every time I think about going near Eno, every time I turn around, Yates has his eyes firmly on me. Even with my back turned I can feel them pressing into the back of my head.

They make me itch too.

'We need a distraction,' I whisper to Malc.

He's painting a lemon green, which just makes it look like a fat lime.

'How?' says Malc.

'Maybe you could pretend to faint or something?'

'Why me?'

'OK, I'll pretend to faint and you can have a pocket full of ants.'

The Schnitzel shudders. 'Fine,' he says. 'But why would I faint?'

I fart.

'Fair enough.'

'You can do it,' I tell him. 'You're a brilliant actor – you've always been the best at getting shot when we play secret agents.'

'True,' he says modestly. 'OK, I'll do it. Agent Schnitzel is going in.'

Malc groans loudly and takes a staggering step away from his desk. 'I don't feel good,' he says.

All heads in the classroom turn towards the

Schnitzel. Including the one belonging to the school inspector.

'Not good how?' asks Mr Gunn.

'Feel . . . dizzy,' says the Schnitzel, and he presses the back of one hand to his forehead.

Some might say that when I told Malc he was a brilliant actor, I might have been . . . stretching the truth.

The regular, unstretched, actual-size truth is: Malc is a *terrible* actor. Whenever we play secret agents, he goes completely over the top – moaning, gasping, staggering, clutching his guts and pirouetting on the spot as many as four times before – finally – falling down 'dead'. But hey, if you can't stretch the truth to save the world, then when can you?

'I think it's all the farts, sir,' says Malcolm, causing a ripple of laughter across the room.

'Back to your desk,' says Mr Gunn, his tone of voice making it clear he is not convinced by the Schnitz's performance.

The school inspector watches Malcolm closely. His eyes narrow. His mouth tightens into a thin line. His nose twitches.

Malc holds out both arms in front of his chest. 'Who said that? Can't see . . .' and he stumbles unconvincingly into Maria Mamooli's desk, knocking her purple pineapple to the floor.

'Stop this silliness, now,' says Mr Gunn.

Malc – one eye closed and one open – staggers forward. He stops next to Eno's desk and turns on the spot – once, twice, three times – before buckling at the knees, bending at the waist, farting and falling – very slowly – to the ground. It's an awful bit of acting, but everyone – Mr Gunn and Mr Yates included – has their attention firmly on the Schnitzel.

Gloria flashes me a quick look: *Do it now!*

A crowd has formed, everyone huddled in and bending over to get a better look at Malcolm.

I move into position behind Eno, take the tube

of bugs from my pocket, pop off the lid and aim the opening at his back pocket.

As if sensing my presence, a red light flashes above the pocket and a voice says: *Please enter password*. With all the commotion happening around Malc, no one hears this but me. There is nowhere to enter a password – no screen or buttons – so I move my face close to Eno's bum.

'Password,' I whisper into the pocket.

The red light flashes on and off: 'Two attempts remaining.'

'Eno Fezzinuff,' I try.

The light blinks on and off: 'One attempt remaining.'

What password would I choose if I was a smug-faced future evil ge—

Of course!

'Genius.'

The light on Eno's back pocket turns from red to green and the pocket pops open about a centimetre.

More than enough. But I'm running out of time.

'That's quite enough now, Mr Schnitzel,' says Mr Gunn. 'Let's get you to your feet. Come now.'

Malcolm yelps. 'Think I might have broken something, sir. Leg maybe.'

'I've seen feathers fall harder,' says the inspector.

'Ouch ouch ouch,' says Malc unconvincingly as he writhes (equally unconvincingly) on the floor.

I have the tube of bugs aimed at Eno's pocket but the bugs aren't budging.

I have an idea.

The bottom of the tube is closed off with a thin disc of cardboard. I use a fingernail to prise this free, opening up the tube so I can see all the way through it. More than this, I can now blow through the tube, launching the bugs directly into Eno's pocket.

I take a deep breath, wrap my lips around the tube and aim it carefully.

I'm about to blow when Mr Gunn claps his hands

and says in a firm voice, 'Everybody back to their desks *now!*'

Eno is – of course – the first to go. As he does he backs into me, shoving the tube halfway into my mouth. Instead of blowing, I gasp. Instead of launching the bugs into his pocket, I inhale them into my mouth.

I scream, which, with the tube in my mouth, comes out sounding like someone shouting for help from the bottom of a very deep cave.

Everyone turns to me.

Si, the inspector, narrows his eyes. 'You,' he says.

Something crawls over my tongue

I scream again, and this time a blizzard of twenty or more ants shoots from the tube and into the air. Except the ants are no ordinary ants – they're the flying kind.

People scream and scatter.

The insects swarm and buzz around the strangely coloured fruit. Children run and panic, desks are turned over and fruit is squished onto the floor.

The inspector takes a step towards me. He stands on a yellow strawberry, slips and falls flat on his bottom.

Behind him, Mr Gunn looks at me with an expression of deep, deep disappointment.

'Detention?' I ask.

Mr Gunn nods. 'Detention.'

I thought all the bugs had taken flight, but something tickles my lips. I put my fingers to my mouth and remove a wriggling ladybird.

Malcolm faints.

It's too much. It's *all* too much.

I get the tingles and then the drags.

A shudder followed by a squish.

And before you can say *ants in his pants*, I'm gone.

ALL HUMANS MUST PICNIC.
BEWARE OF THE CAKE.
BEWARE OF THE ELECTRIC FENCE.
FLYING ROBOT ANTS.

Here's a thing about time travelling into the future:

There's a lot to take in.

Think about where you are right now – what can you see? Who else is around? Is it hot or cold? Are there any smells? Is there a clock ticking, traffic noise, an argument in another room? Maybe you're reading in bed, on a bus, on a beach, in a classroom. Wherever you are now, that place is crammed with details, some of which are familiar, others you notice a bit at a time, *over* time. But when you time travel you're dropped slap bang into the middle of a strange place and time. It's . . . it's a lot to take in.

The first thing I notice now is that we're outside.

And that has to be a good thing, right?

I'm sitting on a red-checked picnic blanket with my future self, my future wife and – a strawberry in his fat little fist – my future son. All three are staring at me as I take in my surroundings and adjust to the future.

I notice that none are wearing electric collars, which is another good sign.

'Bobo,' says the baby. He's strapped into a baby bouncer, with a tub of strawberries in his lap. There's more food set out on the blanket – fruit, chicken, sandwiches, a cake.

I smell popcorn too, but I can't see any.

'Excuse me,' says Future Me.

'That's disgusting,' I tell him.

'Nice to see you too.' And – *annoying!* – he ruffles my hair.

'Bobo,' says the baby – says *my son* – holding a strawberry out to me.

I mutter a thank you, take the strawberry and pop it into my mouth.

'I think he likes you,' says Gloria.

'That's handy,' says Future Me. 'What with Bob being his dad.'

They laugh, but it's one of those polite laughs. If anything, I'd say they looked sad.

I glance around.

We're in the fields close to the woods, and other families are picnicking too. All sitting on identical picnic blankets, all with identical hampers and, from what I can see, identical picnics. The park has changed in the twenty-six years since I was last here – there's a new climbing frame, a slide in the shape of a snake and some sort of giant clown head that's probably a den or something. It looks cool, although no one is playing on any of it.

'Looks like everything worked out,' I say.

But something feels strange – the identical picnic blankets, the high fence surrounding the park, and the uncomfortable silence in response to my words.

'Didn't it?' I say.

Future Bob shakes his head and a tear rolls down Future Glo's face.

'Beebee,' says my son, holding out another strawberry. At least he seems happy.

'It's worse,' says Future Me, keeping his voice low. 'Much worse.'

Gloria sniffs back a tear and picks up the baby from his bouncer, cuddling him close to her chest and kissing his fluffy hair. The baby farts.

'Does he have farting flu?' I ask.

'No,' says Gloria. 'But those little jars of baby food he eats give him awful wind.'

At the mention of food – even baby food – my tummy rumbles.

'Before you tell me what's going on,' I say, 'any chance I could have a piece of that cake?'

Future Bob slides the cake out of my reach. 'Stick to the strawberries,' he says. 'Trust me.'

I take a strawberry.

'Si is more controlling than ever,' says Future Me. 'New measures are brought in almost every week. We eat when and what Si says we eat. We sleep when we're told, work when we're told and exercise when Si says we exercise.'

'Exercise?'

'Burpees.'

'They're the worst!'

'I know,' says Future Me. 'We do one hundred every morning. *Everything* we do is controlled by Si.'

'But . . .' I gesture around the park, 'it looks like everyone's having a nice time.'

'Today is *picnic day*,' says Gloria with a forced smile.

'Everyone picnics for exactly one hour twice a

week,' says Future Me. 'Doesn't matter if it's hot or cold or pouring with rain.'

And that's when I notice the rain. A large parasol is suspended over our heads (there is no pole supporting it, which is pretty cool) but the rain is coming down hard and the edges of the picnic blanket are damp.

'Why?' I ask.

'All humans must picnic,' says Gloria, in a passable impression of Si.

'Because Si has decided that picnicking – like having sing-songs, weaving baskets and reading poetry – are the kinds of "decent, wholesome activities" humans should do.'

'Why would it think that?'

'Ever heard people talk about the *good old days*?'

'I might have heard Granddad say it once.'

'It's something grown-ups say. Like "When I was young we never had all these gadgets," or "When I was a lad we used to play with sticks."'

'"When I was a girl, we used to eat all our vegetables,"' says Gloria.

'When I was a boy I used to get up at six thirty in the morning to do a paper round,' I say.

'Exactly,' says Future Me. 'Well, as many times as you've heard it, Si – because it's *everywhere* – must have heard it billions of times. This idea that things were somehow better in the past.'

'From where I'm sitting, it might be right,' I say.

'But not all progress is bad,' says Future Me. 'And everything from the past is not automatically *better.*'

'Technology can be great,' says Gloria.

'And playing with sticks is rubbish,' says Future Me.

'Although you probably should eat your vegetables,' says Gloria.

'It's all about balance,' says Future Me. 'The thing is, no matter how much it reads, watches or learns, Si doesn't know what it means to be human and happy any more than we know what it means to be a line of code. Frankly, I think it's gone the computer equivalent of insane.'

'Is that why you look so awful?' I ask.

'Awful?' says Gloria, looking offended.

'Tired?' I try.

'Oh that's just part of being a parent,' says Future Me. 'Your baby boy likes to get up at least twice in the middle of every night. It's exhausting.'

'Wouldn't be so bad if we could take a nap during the day,' says Gloria, 'but Si doesn't allow naps. He'd rather we played snap or arranged flowers.'

'Why haven't you run off to the forest?' I say. 'I would.'

Gloria glances towards the high fence surrounding the park. 'It's not so easy, any more.'

'There are patrols, for one thing.'

'Patrols?'

'Droids. If they catch you, it's . . . well, no more picnics.'

'Meaning?'

'They send you to a work colony,' says Future Me.

'Doing what?'

'Making patrol droids,' says Gloria.

'Right. But, maybe they won't catch you.' I glance towards the woods bordering the park. I'm not the fastest runner, but I think I could make it in under a minute. And the fence isn't so high that I couldn't climb over it.

Future Me has followed my eyes and read my mind. He shakes his head.

I'm about to ask why, when I hear someone shout.

A man jumps up from his picnic blanket. 'I can't take it any more!' he shouts, and sets off running towards the woods.

'Yes!' I say.

But Future Bob holds his finger to his lips and shushes me.

The man is perhaps a quarter of the way to the fence when a siren wails into life and a voice booms across the field: 'This is Si,' says the voice. 'Do not approach the fence.'

Red lights flash at intervals along the length of the fence, and beneath the grey sky the wire crackles with a faint blue glow of electricity. The man keeps running.

'He'll get electrocuted!' I say.

'Probably,' says Future Me.

The sky booms with thunder. My baby son whimpers and Gloria rocks him in her arms and whispers shushing noises into his tiny ear.

The man is closing in on the fence. He reaches into his back pocket and pulls on a pair of yellow gloves.

'Washing-up gloves,' says Future Me. 'Clever.'

'Why?'

'To insulate his hands from the electricity,' he says.

'Won't do him any good though,' says Gloria.

Lightning flashes across the sky and strikes the fence.

'Final warning,' says Si.

The man keeps running.

A squeal of metal draws my attention to the playground. The climbing frame is moving – rising out of the ground, twisting, unfolding, reorganising its rails and rungs into what look like legs. Two at first, then another two and another and . . .

'A spider,' I say. 'Is that a gigantic metal spider?'

'Patrol droid,' says Gloria. 'And it's an ant.'

'A flying ant,' says Future Me, and there is a note of guilt in his voice.

The patrol droid sprouts a pair of wings, rises into the air and swivels to face the fleeing man. He's maybe twenty steps away from the fence. There's still a chance he can–

But no.

In the space of a single heartbeat, the flying ant zooms across the field and draws level with the man. The droid extends two legs and grabs hold of the man. Somewhere on a picnic blanket a woman gasps.

'Return to your picnics!' says the voice of Si. 'Enjoy your picnics!'

The droid rises into the air and flies into the distance, disappearing into the dark clouds and thunder.

'Happens every time,' says Future Me, shaking his head sadly.

'Does anyone ever make it?'

'Not that we've ever seen,' says Gloria.

'What if you just . . . you know, snuck. Instead of running screaming towards the fence.'

'Wouldn't make any difference,' says Gloria. 'Everyone contains nanobots now.'

'Tiny robot bugs?' I say.

'More or less,' says Future Me. 'Si sneaks them into the food. Cake, mostly.'

'They trigger the patrol droids when you get within fifteen metres of the fence.'

I glance back to the playground. 'The droid's gone,' I say. 'You could make it if you went now.'

Gloria nods towards the playground. 'That clown,' she says. 'And the slide that looks like a snake.'

'Patrol droids,' says Future Me.

'Si sure does like its robots,' I say.

'All the better to control us with,' says Future Me.

'But why would you have a patrol droid shaped like a clown?' I ask.

'They're based on common phobias,' says Gloria.

'Fears,' says Future Me.

I roll my eyes at him. 'I know what phobias are. I didn't know people were scared of clowns though.'

Gloria shudders. 'They give me the creeps.'

'Enough about phobias,' says Future Me. 'You'll be dragged back to the past any moment now, and we have something we need you to do first, so pay attention.'

BOB AND ELVIS GO FOR A WALK.
HERE COME THE DROIDS.
A DISAPPOINTING BUNNY.

Future Me glances at the electric fence.

I follow his eyes and the top of the fence thrums and fizzes with blue sparks. 'What? No. No way.'

'Calm down,' says Future Me. 'It's very important you stay calm. Elvis's future depends on it.'

'Elvis? You named our son after . . . you named him after Dad?'

Future Me nods. 'What do you think?'

'I like it,' I say. 'Yeah. I like it a lot.'

'OK, listen. You're going to take Elvis to the fence.'

'But it's electric!!'

'Calm, Bob,' he says in a soothing tone. 'If you get excited you might get the tingles and you won't be any use to our son then.'

'But it's electric,' I say in my calmest voice.

'You won't have to touch it. When you get there, a squad of wild folk will be on the other side. They'll throw a rubber sheet over the fence, someone will climb over and take you and Elvis to safety.'

'How do you know? How do you know they'll be there?'

'I've been talking to them,' says Future Me. 'I've been talking to Malcolm.'

'On the walkie? I thought –'

'He leaves notes,' says Future Me.

'And Si allows that?'

'Si doesn't know. I was visiting Mum's grave a few months back. I had flowers, and when I took away the old ones, I found a note hidden in the stems. He sneaks in there at night. There are no droids in the graveyard.

Not yet, anyway. So I scribbled a reply and hid it under the fresh flowers. We've been talking that way for weeks.'

'But how did you know I'd be here today?'

'I didn't, but we bring Elvis to the climbing frames most days, and with the picnics on top of that we figured – hoped – you'd show up sooner or later. And –' he ruffles my hair again – 'here you are.'

It's still annoying, but I let it go.

'What about you?' I say. 'Can't you come too?'

Gloria is crying.

Future Me says, 'You saw what happened to that guy.'

'But Elvis needs you.'

'It's just temporary, just until you fix the future,' says Future Me, and I get the sense that he is saying this as much for Gloria's benefit as mine. 'It happened during World War II.'

'What? Robot ants?'

'Sending children to a place of safety,' says Future Me. 'It happened to our great-granddad, apparently.'

Gloria's tears have turned into full-on sobbing now and I feel that if she keeps it up I'm going to cry too, and there's no way I'm doing that!

'Talking of robot ants,' I say, 'what happens if one comes after me?'

'Hopefully they won't,' says Future Me.

'Hopefully?!'

'We're going to distract them,' says Gloria.

'How?'

'By running for the fence,' says Future Me.

'But, the droids . . . they'll come for you.'

'Exactly. And while all eyes are on us, you will walk – slowly and calmly – to that oak tree over there.'

I'm rubbish at trees. I only know conker trees, Christmas trees and – because there's one near Mum's grave – sycamore trees. But Future Me, of course, knows this.

'It's the one with the yellow ribbon tied to the trunk,' he says. 'Make your way there, and Malcolm will be waiting on the other side. As soon as we activate the droids, he'll be looking out for you.'

Now Future Me turns to Gloria. 'It's time,' he says.

She strokes baby Elvis's hair, and the tears are streaming down her cheeks now. 'I'm scared,' she says.

'Me too,' says Future Me, kissing her on the forehead. 'But Bob's going to save the world for us, aren't you, Bob?'

'Yes,' I say. 'I'll save the world.'

I try to sound confident and brave and capable, but to my ears I fail on all three counts.

Future Me lifts Elvis from his mother's arms and holds him out to me. I've never held a baby but I've seen it done, and I cradle his body with one hand and support his head with the other. I'm amazed at how light he is. How warm and soft and . . . amazing.

'You keep our baby safe,' says Gloria. 'OK?'

'OK,' I say, and there is a lump in my throat.

'I'm going left,' says Future Me. 'Glo is going right. When the droids move in, that's your signal to go. Walk at a steady pace, try to stay calm.'

Baby Elvis reaches up and touches my face. Then he pulls gently on my nose, and when he smiles – despite everything else – I smile too.

'OK,' says Future Me, rising to his feet. 'Let's get this show on the road.'

Gloria leans across and kisses Elvis. And then she kisses me. It's weird, because I don't even mind.

'I love you,' says Gloria.

She says it to the baby, but I feel that a bit of it is aimed at me too.

'See you in the future,' says Future Me.

I nod. 'See you in the future.'

And without another word they both start walking. They walk in straight lines, staying parallel to the fence but not approaching it. Yet. Rain lashes down on them, but they walk tall and unhunched, like people with a purpose.

I count thirty steps before a voice echoes across the park:

'Return to your picnic blankets, please.'

My baby chuckles in my arms. I don't feel much like laughing but I force a smile for Elvis's sake.

Gloria and Future Me continue walking. Five or six more paces, then:

'Return to your picnic blankets. NOW.'

They turn to face each other. Future Me blows a kiss across the stretch of grass that separates them; Gloria catches it, holds it to her lips for a second then begins running for the fence.

A siren wails, red lights flash on top of the metal posts, and the voice booms:

'This is Si. Do not approach the fence.'

But, of course, they do.

And here come the droids.

The snake rears up, hisses a forked metal tongue at the clouds and slithers rapidly in the direction of my future self. The clown head blinks its eyes, its nose flashes red and the gigantic, jolly, terrifying metal ball starts rolling across the field towards Gloria.

Elvis laughs.

'That's our cue,' I say to my son, and I get to my feet and start walking directly for the fence.

The snake droid has caught up with Future Me and trapped him in its thick metal coils. Future Me screams.

Elvis begins to cry. 'Dada. Dada.'

I feel my heart rate jump and that's not a good thing. I can't afford to get the tingles now. 'It's OK,' I whisper to the baby. And I say it again – *It's OK* – to myself.

But it really isn't.

The clown rolls level with Gloria and its eyes pop out on long springs. The springs surround Gloria, penning her in like a trapped animal.

'Mama,' says Elvis.

'Yes,' I say. 'Mama's having fun with the clown.'

The clown's springs start to pull tight now, closing in on Gloria and drawing her towards its grinning face. At the same time, the snake opens its jaws wide and swallows Future Me whole. His screams are muffled and metallic as the mouth snaps shut and the snake slithers into the distance.

My skin fizzes, and I try taking deep slow breaths to calm myself and hold back the tingles, but I won't be able to hold them for long. I focus on the fence and keep walking. And now, from the other side of the fence a bunch of figures emerge from behind the oak tree – they're dressed in ragged clothes, their skin is dirty and the men are bearded. But I immediately recognise Future Malc at the head of this group. He sees me and waves. I wave back.

I look over my shoulder in time to see the clown head lift into the air. The clown's bow tie is spinning like a propeller and I stand motionless for a moment, watching as it helicopters into the clouds and away.

Calm thoughts, I think, *calm thoughts.*

But it's not easy with all these flashing lights, sirens and terrifying droids. I try imagining a fluffy bunny, but in my mind's eye the bunny is transformed into a sharp-toothed droid with propellers for ears.

'Bob!' shouts a voice, and I come back to my senses.

The wild folk have thrown what must be the rubber sheet over the fence and Malc sits on top of this, waving me towards him. I continue walking – quickly but not quite running – breathing deep and whispering shushing noises to Elvis and to myself.

My legs are wobbly and I have the full-body feeling of pins and needles that is the tingles.

'Do not approach the fence!' says the voice of Si.

I risk a backwards glance and see a small buzzing speck approaching through the clouds. The flying-ant droid has returned. Time – as it tends to do – is running out.

I focus all my attention on the fence and the waiting free folk, I concentrate all my efforts on putting one foot in front of the other. I'm close now, but everything is fuzzing out.

'STEP AWAY FROM THE FENCE!'

I take a step and stumble. I drop to one knee but keep a tight hold on Elvis.

A shadow falls over me and I don't need to look up to know it's the flying robot ant. I force myself to my feet.

The tingles have been replaced by the drags and it feels like I'm wading through syrup, but I take one more step.

My vision blurs and I have seconds at the most. Another step and I bump into something soft and rubbery. I'm at the fence.

A figure reaches down to me and a voice says, 'Give me the baby, Bob. I'll take it from here.'

Baby Elvis is lifted from my arms.

Something metallic grabs one of my legs. It pulls me back from the fence, but the machine is too late. The drags have a firmer grip than any robot and I'm dragged out of the future and backwards through time.

INSECT FIREWORKS.
DETENTION. AGAIN.
NO TIME FOR NIT-PICKING.
YET ANOTHER AWFUL JOB.

That was a rough one.

I can still feel the baby warmth on my chest where I held Elvis. That was the first time I ever held my son and I . . . I think I miss him.

And I'm worried for Future Me and Future Glo. I don't know what's happening to them 'out there' – are they stuck in some future where they're separated from their child and working in a labour camp building droids? Or are they . . . nowhere . . . waiting for the future, whatever it is, to catch up with them?

Well, one thing's for sure – there will be no nanobots and no flying droids if I have anything to do with it.

Which brings me back to the present.

To Mr Gunn's classroom.

I have a Smarties tube full of insects in my mouth and Eno's bum about twelve centimetres in front of my face. If I'd arrived here ten seconds later the room would be full of buzzing insects, but I have a chance now to stop that happening.

I step away from Eno, replace the lid on the tube of bugs and slide it into my own back pocket. Above the bodies of my bent-over classmates, I catch Malcolm's eye and shake my head.

He frowns.

I glance towards our desks and make a 'get up' gesture with my hands.

Another frown.

I mouth the words *New plan*.

Malc is about to frown for a third time, when

Gloria – who has been watching this exchange – kneels down beside him and says: 'I imagine you're feeling better now.'

'Oh, am I?' says Malc, looking from Gloria to me.

I nod.

'Great,' says the Schnitzel, getting to his feet. 'Sorry about that Mr Gunn, all better now.'

Mr Gunn does not look convinced, and Mr Yates gives me a long, suspicious stare. We return to our desks and I can feel the inspector's eyes following me every step of the way.

'What happened?' says Malc.

I don't even know where to begin. My body is tired and my mind is spinning.

I sit down heavily, and immediately realise my mistake.

The Smarties tube is suddenly squashed between my bum and the seat, there is a short sharp *Pop!* and the lid flies off the tube and across the classroom. This is followed a moment later by a greenfly, a ladybird and a small army of flying ants. It's as if someone – me – has set off an insect firework.

The bugs swarm over the room, people scream, desks are tipped over and multicoloured fruit is trampled underfoot. In the midst of it all, Mr Yates stares only at me.

He takes a step forward and – before I have a chance to warn him – slips on a turquoise raspberry and lands on his bum with a painful thud. Like the various pieces of painted fruit, Mr Yate's face undergoes a colour change, in his case from peachy pink to strawberry red.

Mr Gunn looks at me and shakes his head.

'Detention?'

'Detention.'

'Two detentions in two days,' says Dad. 'What are you doing, going for a world record?'

It's good that he can still joke about it, and I laugh.

'Not a joke,' says Dad.

'Oh, sorry.'

After I accidentally set off the bug firework, Mr Gunn talked to Mrs Gren, who is also our form tutor, and Mrs G said that me and Malc and Gloria weren't allowed to sit with each other for the rest of the day. We didn't even get to talk at lunchtime because I was in detention with Mr Gunn. And then, at the end of the day, Mrs Gren held me back for another 'talk'.

Are you sure everything is OK? she asked. *You're sure there's nothing going on you want to talk about?*

I told her I was fine.

I would understand, Mrs Gren told me. *You've been through a lot.*

I know! I thought. *Like trying to save the world!*

But that wasn't what Mrs G meant. She was talking about Mum again. So I told her I was fine, again.

Mrs G nodded like she understood and gave me another jammy dodger.

Dad, on the other hand, has not got the biscuits out.

'You're not a bad boy,' he says. '*I* know that. But first the volcano and now this nonsense with the wasps.'

'Ants,' I say. 'Flying an—'

Dad is giving me a look that says this is no time for nit-picking.

Or would that be gnat-picking?

Under the table, Zem curls up at my feet and lets out a sigh. I like to think he's there for moral support, but the truth is Zem likes hanging out under the table because he can usually find a dropped morsel of whatever Dad and I last ate. Based on how awful Dad's cooking is, and how smelly Zem's farts are, we probably shouldn't encourage this kind of behaviour. But it does save us from having to clean the floor quite so often.

'It was an accident,' I say to Dad. 'I didn't mean to set them loose.'

'And yet you did. Why did you even have a pocket full of . . . ants?'

I shrug.

'Is that the best you can do, Bob? A shrug?'

I nod.

'Fine,' he says. 'Have you got any homework?'

'No.'

'In that case you can clean the cobwebs out of the garage.'

'But there's hundreds of them!'

'That's why they need cleaning. And while you're in there, have a good think about how you're carrying on.'

I bet Superman or Batman never had to clean cobwebs from the garage when *they* were trying to save the world. Although it probably happened quite regularly for Spider-Man.

COBWEBS!
A CHAT WITH MRS DIZZ.
ALL THEM TRUMPETS.

Cobwebs!

They stick to everything – my fingers, my face, my neck, my hair. I have cobwebs in my eyelashes, in my mouth and in my pockets.

Judging by how many cobwebs I have cleaned in the last hour– approximately one million – it seems every spider in the country has at some point visited our garage and had a party. There were cobwebs in every corner and on every shelf. Cobwebs on the walls, ceiling, door and floor.

I'm going to say cleaning cobwebs is even more

revolting than cleaning up Zem's poos – at least you don't get them all over your clothes.

It should be a swearword. You stub your toe on the edge of the bed: *Cobwebs.* Forget to do your homework: *Cobwebs!* Try to save the world and end up making things even worse: *Cobwebs!!*

The worst thing, though, is that I really don't have time for this. I need a plan and I need it quick. If not for the sake of all humanity, then for my baby. I know that sounds all backwards, but I guess that's how being a dad feels. Unless I'm doing that wrong too.

At least the garage is clean.

Although as clean as it is, I am dirty.

I have the garage door open and a gentle rain is falling outside. I put down my broom and step out into the drizzle. Eyes closed, I tilt my face to the sky, letting the rain wash over me and rinse some of the yuck from my hair.

'Nice night for it,' says a voice. I recognise it straight

away as Gloria's mum, thanks to her strong Jamaican accent.

'Evening, Mrs Dizamale.'

She is standing at the top of her driveway, an umbrella in one hand and a kitchen bin held under the other arm.

'Want some help with that?'

'You're a good boy,' says Mrs Dizz. 'You can help me sort the paper and plastic.'

At that moment I notice that she has a bunch of flowers – roses, I think – hanging out of the neck of her jumper. I'm about to ask why when Mrs Dizz sets down the pedal bin and farts.

'Pardon, Bob. I think I've got a tummy bug.'

'There's seems to be a lot of it going around,' I say.

'You look a fright,' she says. 'What's happening?'

I grab a handful of cardboard and drop it into the blue box.

'Been cleaning cobwebs.'

'Your dad punish you for acting up?'

'Sorry for squashing Gloria's volcano,' I say. 'It was an accident.'

'They happen,' says Mrs Dizz. 'To some more than others.' And she winks at me. 'But they happen.'

Mrs Dizz tilts her umbrella so that it covers both of us and we just stand silently for a while, sorting the recycling and listening to the patter of rain above our heads.

Mrs Dizz pauses and says, 'And is everything OK with you, Bob?'

When will people stop asking me if I'm OK?

I answer my own thought:

When you stop diving on volcanoes and releasing insects into classrooms.

'I'm fine,' I tell her, and I reach into the bottom of the pedal bin for the last of the recycling.

Mrs Dizz looks at me as if deciding whether or not to accept my answer. 'You'll come for supper one night,' she says. There is no question mark on the end. 'Give your dad a night off.'

'OK.'

'You like goat?'

My face drops and Mrs Dizz laughs. 'You will,' she says. And she pinches me gently around the upper arm. 'Put some meat on you.'

'Can I ask a question?'

'Yes, Bob.'

'Why have you got a bunch of flowers in your jumper?'

'All them trumpets,' she says.

'Guffs?'

Mrs Dizz laughs her big loud laugh. 'Exactly. And Mr Dizamale, let me tell you, his trumpets are powerful things. But' – she waggles her flowers – 'all I can smell is roses.'

'Brilliant,' I say.

And it might just be. Not sticking flowers down your

jumper – that's bonkers – but Mrs Dizz has just given me an idea. The idea is also bonkers. But that doesn't mean it can't work.

'Now go an' get yourself out of this rain,' says Mrs Dizz. 'And make sure you come for supper soon. Gloria will like that.'

'I will. Thank you.'

And I head inside for a very long, very hot shower.

MIDNIGHT MEETING AT
SCHNITZEL'S EMPORIUM.

I think I have the answer. It came to me in a flash while Mrs Dizz was talking about her husband's powerful bum trumpets. Although I suppose the idea has been brewing ever since my first jolt into the year 2046. Ever since Future Me said that the best thing about the smart trousers was the fart filters. That they are what encouraged Mr Schnitzel to sell the silly things in his shop.

So my idea is this:

If we can convince people the fart filters don't work,

Mr Schnitzel will never stock the trousers, Sandra Katana's dad will never take a pair to Japan, and the trousers will be forgotten about before you can say 'Who made that awful smell?'

It's ten past bedtime and I can hear Dad watching a film downstairs. Something with explosions and guns and car chases, which means I should be able to talk to Malc without Dad hearing me.

I wait for an explosion and slide my window open. 'Malc.'

A second later his window opens. 'Are you OK?' he asks. 'What did your dad say about you getting detention again?'

'Made me clean all the cobwebs out of garage. It was gross.'

'Should have walkied me,' Malc says. 'I'd have come over.'

'Walkie's not working. I think it needs new batteries. Anyway, thank you.'

'What for?'

'For saying you'd have come over. It would've been good to have some help.'

'Oh, I wasn't offering to help. I just thought it sounded funny.'

Hmmm.

'Still,' says the Schnitz, 'at least we saved the world.'

Thanks to being separated for the rest of the day at school, this is the first chance we've had to talk since I released flying ants all over Mr Gunn's classroom.

'Right . . . ?' says Malc, but he's seen the expression on my face and that *right* doesn't sound very confident.

I shake my head. 'Not exactly.'

'*Not exactly?* What does that mean?'

'We might have made things a tiny bit worse.'

'How tiny?'

There is a moment of quiet in the film downstairs and I wait before answering. A burst of machine-gun fire thunders up through the floorboards.

I continue: 'Depends on what you think of flying robot ants.'

'Never seen one,' says Malc. 'And I hope I never do. So what now? Breakfast meeting?'

'We can't wait. This,' I say, 'calls for a . . . midnight meeting.'

Gloria's window opens. 'Brilliant. Are we making a new plan then?'

'Already made one,' I say. 'Schnitz, can you get us into your dad's shop?'

He looks like I've just asked him if we can steal a car. 'Why?'

'We need to . . . borrow some supplies.'

'I don't know,' says Malc. 'I could, I suppose, but isn't that a bit . . . naughty?'

'Maybe. Kind of. Possibly. But it's only so we can save the world.'

'I'm in,' says Gloria.

'It's not your dad's shop,' says Malc.

'Come on,' I say. 'Yesterday you were talking about blowing up the internet. This is nothing compared to that.'

Schnitz thinks about this.

There is a warm breeze blowing this evening, which is a good thing, considering what I have in mind.

'Are you sure the world is in danger? You're not . . .' he looks guilty, 'making this up. For fun?' There's a pause. Then he says, 'Sorry.'

'Don't be,' I say. 'I wouldn't believe me either. But all I can do is ask you to tr—'

'I trust you,' says the Schnitzel. 'See you outside at midnight.'

'This is exciting,' says Gloria.

'If we get caught, we'll be grounded until we're a hundred,' says Malcolm.

'At least.'

20

EXIT THROUGH THE DOG FLAP.
PIRATES.
MIDNIGHT FEAST TO
SAVE THE WORLD.
FART BALLOONS.

Everything is quiet and still.

I can hear Dad snoring in his room, but even this seems only to highlight the silence. Every footstep I take sounds like a dropped rock, and even though I know I'm imagining it, I expect Dad to wake at any moment.

Getting down the creaky stairs is the easy part. The hard part is getting out of the house.

Dad locks the front door and back door at night and both are connected to an alarm. I could turn the alarm off – the code is my birthday – but the control panel beeps when you punch in each number, then does one long ten-second beep to tell you the alarm has been set or unset. There's no way it wouldn't wake Dad.

So I do what any half-decent secret agent would do.

I wriggle through Zem's dog flap. Zem is a medium-sized dog and a little 'comfy' around the middle, but even so, it's a tight squeeze and I have a brief moment of panic where I think I'm going to get stuck with my bum in the kitchen and my head outside. But with a little more wriggling, worming and squirming, I make it through and out into midnight.

I'm free.

This is going to work.

When I make my way down the side path to the front garden, Malcolm and Gloria are waiting for me, sitting on the front wall in their pyjamas like we do this kind of thing all the time.

'Suits you,' says Gloria, as we set off walking to Schnitzel's Emporium.

'What suits me? Creeping about in the middle of the night?'

She puts a hand to my head. 'The headscarf.'

I figured if there was even a tiny chance it might stop me from going bald, I should try sleeping in it. I'd intended to take the scarf off before leaving the house, but I was so worried about getting caught by Dad, I completely forgot about it.

'Makes you look like a pirate,' says Malc.

I blush in embarrassment, but luckily it's so dark no one notices.

'Trebor the Terrible,' says Gloria.

Which, I have to admit, is a pretty good pirate name.

'What does that make you then?' I say.

'Dead-Eye Dizamale,' says Malc.

'Sounds more like a cowboy name,' says Glo.

'Roaring Gloria?' I try.

'Arr, I like that!' says Gloria in her best pirate voice.

'Do me!' says Malc.

'You be Salty Seadog Schnitzel,' I tell him. 'Deadliest man to sail the seas.'

'Aye,' agrees Schnitzel, 'that be me.'

'So,' says Roaring Gloria. 'What be our mission this cold night?'

'Arr,' says the Seadog. 'Tell us, what future horrors did ye spy in the seas of time?'

And just like that – at the mention of the word 'future' – I am soaked in freezing-cold reality and this pirate game feels kind of silly. I am no longer Trebor the Terrible; I am simply Bob. A twelve-year-old accidental time traveller with a future to save and not much time to do it.

Which, when you put it like that, is actually pretty cool. Perhaps even as cool as being a pirate.

And so, as we walk through the quiet streets, I tell my friends about the future. About the compulsory picnics, the nanobots, the electric fence and the droids. I leave out the bit about me and Gloria having a baby and evacuating it to the forest. For one, it's too weird. For two, I feel that if I talk about Elvis I might cry. It's very strange.

Schnitzel's Emporium is a short walk from our houses, and I've just finished explaining my idea to sabotage the fart filters when we arrive at the shop.

'So how are we going to do it?' asks Malc.

'We're going to have a midnight feast,' I say. 'Open the shop and I'll explain.'

Schnitzel's Emporium is a maze constructed from shelves, and because Mr Schnitz is always adding new items, it looks different every time you enter. There are boxes in the aisles, items hanging from the ceiling, and the place really should come with a map. A boy got lost in here once for most of a Saturday, and they only found him when he fell into a box full of bicycle bells, which he rang constantly until help arrived. Or at least that's what everyone says.

Looking around the shelves now, I spot jigsaw puzzles and vegetables, rubber boots and fruits, dishes and pans and potted plants, sacks of gravel and packets of crisps, stacks of fizzy drinks, a wheelbarrow, a tent, cleaning products, baby products, baby-cleaning products, coils of rope, balls of wool, various hats, children's scooters and a whole section of novelty items like whoopee cushions, fake poos and sweets that dye your mouth blue.

And that's just the stuff I can *see*.

Today it also has a display of Father's Day cards, which reminds me of two things:

1) I need to make a Father's Day card between now and Sunday.

2) I am a father in the future and I need to save the world for – among several billion others – my baby.

Not that I really need reminding of either. But as soon as we're inside the Emporium, I waste no time explaining the plan.

In two words, the plan is this: Fart sacks.

'Fart sacks?' says the Schnitzel.

'Does your dad sell balloons?'

Malc nods.

'Thought so. Great. We trap as many farts as possible in balloons, we fit the balloons with rubber tubes like the ones you used on Harry Snotter, and block the ends with corks. There are our fart sacks. Next we hide the balloons up our jumpers and feed the tubes down our sleeves. Then – whenever Eno farts, or even when he doesn't – we remove the cork from one of the tubes, aim it at Eno and give the fart sack a squeeze.'

'Like in Spider-Man?' says Malcolm.

'Exactly. But instead of slinging web, we're firing farts. Everyone will think it's Eno.'

'So we have to fart into balloons?' says Gloria.

'Correct.'

'Cool.'

'You said we were having a midnight feast,' says Malc.

'We need fart fuel,' I say. 'We have to eat as much farty food as possible.'

'I'm already a bit farty,' says Gloria.

'Me too,' says the Schnitz.

'Yes, but I – the world – needs you a lot farty.'

'Beans?' says Malc.

'Definitely.'

'But we have nowhere to cook them.'

'We'll eat them cold,' I say. 'The future of the world depends on it.'

'Courgettes,' says Gloria. 'They always give me the pops.'

'I hate courgettes,' says Malc.

'Me too, but –'

'I know,' says Malc. 'Future of the world.'

'How about popping candy?' says Gloria.

'Has to work,' I say. 'I mean, it even has "pop" in the name.'

'That's more like it,' says Malc. 'What else?'

I pull a piece of paper from my pyjamas. 'I've made a list.'

We tear the list into three pieces, each take a basket and set off shopping.

FILK

YURPS.

FIVE FINGERS OF GUFF.

A CONVERSATION WITH ZEM.

Ten minutes later, this is what we have: two courgettes, a jar of peanut butter, eight tins of beans, a large bottle of lemonade, two pints of milk, two egg-mayonnaise sandwiches, a bag of dried apricots, a bag of raisins, four packets of popping candy and sixteen jars of baby food in assorted flavours.

Also: a tin opener, a knife, four spoons, a stack of paper cups and a pile of paper plates.

Also also: a pack of party balloons, a bag of elastic bands, three rolls of sticky tape, a tangle of rubber tubing and a bag of corks.

We sit on a stack of cushions at the back of the store with the food laid out between us.

Malc picks up the packet of egg sandwiches. 'These are out of date today,' he says.

'It's only been today for three quarters of an hour,' I point out. 'They'll be fine.'

'Baby food?' says Gloria. 'I didn't know baby food gave you farts.'

I remember baby Elvis's awful guffs in the year 2049. 'Trust me,' I say. 'It does.'

Gloria pops the lid off a jar of 'spinach and orange' baby food; she dips her finger into the orange gloop and tastes it. 'Not bad.'

And then her smart watch says, 'Excuse Me.'

'Stupid thing,' says Gloria. 'It's still connected to Eno's fart trousers. He must have parped in his sleep.'

'No more time to waste,' I say. 'Let's get eating.'

Malc goes straight for the popping candy, I start by opening a tin of beans and Gloria continues eating baby food with her finger.

'It's important that we eat some of everything,' I say.

'Even the courgette?' groans the Schnitzel.

'It's not just about farting,' I say, 'but about farting big. We need all the gas we can get. So yes, everyone has everything.'

Malc empties the entire packet of popping candy into his mouth and reaches for an egg sandwich.

'Fine,' he says. And because his mouth is full of exploding candy, the word is full of crackles and echoes and he sounds like a robot.

We swallow cold beans and dip slices of courgette in peanut butter. We chew apricots and toss raisins into each other's mouths. We eat stale egg sandwiches and spoon down jar after jar of baby food, and Malc adds fizzy lemonade to milk to create *filk*. Which is as horrible as it sounds.

We eat and drink it all, and then we go back for more.

We try bananas, pickled onions and crisps made

from lentils. We even add a spoon of baking power to the *filk*.

By one thirty in the morning, our tummies are swollen and our mouths confused at the clashing flavours.

Gloria finishes a pot of baby food and puts down the spoon. 'If you were washed up on a desert island,' she says, 'and you could only eat one meal until you were rescued, what would it be? Mine would be spicy goat curry with black-eye beans and roti.'

'What's roti?' says Malc.

'Like bread but flatter.'

'How would you make the bread?' I ask.

'Or . . . you know . . . kill the goat?' adds Malcolm.

Gloria shakes her head. 'Imagine you were washed up with a big container full of food. Not ingredients, but like a single meal, already prepared. All you have to do is warm it up on a camp fire.'

'What if you can't make fire?' asks Malc.

'For goodness sake,' says Gloria. 'It's a *game*. If you were on a desert island and could only eat one thing for breakfast, lunch and tea, what would it be?'

'You'd have goat curry for breakfast?' I ask.

Gloria nods. 'Better than having toast for supper.'

I'm not sure I agree; I quite like toast, and if you had enough of it maybe you could build a shelter out of it. Or even a raft.

'Christmas dinner,' says Malc. 'With turkey, roasties, stuffing, honey carrots, gravy and loads of those sausages wrapped in bacon. My mum makes the *best* Christmas dinner.'

Two years ago I would have challenged Malcolm on his last point. But two years ago my mum was still alive. Since we lost her – more than a year ago now – I have had one birthday and one Christmas and neither were the same without Mum. I could write a list one hundred pages long about the things I miss about her, and the longer Mum's gone, the longer the list grows. I don't know where her cooking would come on that list, but I think in the first ten pages for sure – everything she cooked was good, but *her* Christmas dinner – no matter what Malc says – was the best in the world. And yes, I know I haven't tasted *every single* Christmas dinner in the world, but some things you just know. You know?

Since Mum died we've had two Mother's Days too, and they might have been the hardest days of all – harder even than her birthday, which Dad and I celebrated with cake. Although 'celebrate' is a funny word to describe crying onto a couple of cupcakes. It's one of the reasons I want to get Dad something special for Father's Day this year. But how am I going to do that with only 18p and some fluff in my piggy bank?

'Bob?' says Gloria, gently.

I suddenly remember where we are. 'Huh?'

'Desert-island food?' she asks.

I want to say my mum's Christmas dinner. But Malc's already said that and it would seem grumpy if I said it too.

'What if we all got washed up together?' I say. 'Then I could choose ice cream and we could share. Or is that cheating?'

Gloria thinks about this and smiles. 'Sounds kind of fun,' she says. 'I'll allow it.'

'Three-Pirate Island,' says the Schnitzel. 'Awesome.'

Gloria yawns, and – as everybody knows – yawns are contagious. When Gloria yawns she sounds like a cat meowing from inside a wardrobe. Malc's yawns sound like an old man in a cave thinking about a crossword clue. Me, I like to think my yawns sound like a proud hippopotamus calling to his family from across a jungle at sunset.

And then – encouraged by the yawns, perhaps – the burps come. Malc first – he's halfway through a yawn when it changes into a deep gurgling belch. It's brilliant. And it turns out yawn-burps (I think the scientific term is 'yurps') are contagious too.

And they're very funny. Within moments we're laughing and yurping and rolling on the floor clutching our tummies. And then I remember what we're doing here.

'Stop,' I say. 'Everybody stop.'

Malc and Gloria look at me with tired, questioning eyes: *What now?*

'We're wasting gas,' I say. 'We're here to parp, not burp, and we're going to need every bit we can get. Try and hold the burps in.'

'I don't know if I can,' says Malc. 'They're bubbling up.'

Gloria clutches at her tummy.

'Just hold them in. Concentrate, and before long they'll have to bubble down instead of up.'

'Clever,' says Gloria, and the way she looks at me – like she's somehow impressed – makes me blush for the second time tonight.

Luckily, my face is turning red from the effort of holding my burps back and no one notices. The same cannot be said for the fart that follows about thirty seconds later. We all notice that.

It's long, loud and it stinks.

The Schnitzel answers with a fart of his own, and Gloria – never one to be left out of a conversation – drops the biggest fart yet.

'OK, everyone. Action stations. Take a balloon each and start filling it full of farts.'

Everyone takes a balloon and a few elastic bands for holding it closed in between farts. And then we each go to a separate aisle of the Emporium so we can fart into our balloons in private. But there is a problem.

Gloria realises it first.

'The opening of the balloons is too small,' she calls from the biscuits aisle. 'I can't get my farts in.'

'Same,' says Malcolm from the breakfast-cereal aisle. 'I'm guffing all over the place but my balloon isn't inflating.'

'Maybe we need to try without our pyjamas,' I say from the cleaning-products aisle. 'Get your bare bum up against the balloon.'

'Already am,' says Malc. 'It's not working.'

No!!

We've snuck out of our houses at midnight, 'borrowed' all sorts of stuff from Mr Schnitzel, eaten the most revolting midnight feast in history and risked being grounded for our entire lives. We can't fail. Not after all of this.

Think. Think. Think . . .

Which is easier said than done when you're standing in the cleaning section of your best friend's dad's shop holding a balloon to your bare bottom. I release another pop and feel it blow across my fingers. It does nothing to the balloon.

I pull up my pyjamas and pace up and down the aisle, trying to think of a solution. I walk past sponges, scrubbers and rubber gloves; washing-up liquid, glass cleaner, toilet cleaner. As I walk, I fiddle with the balloon, stretching it and snapping it and pulling it over the tip of my finger so it looks like it's been whacked with a hammer.

I stop walking.

I look at the balloon on my finger and something about it tickles at my brain. I walk backwards down the aisle, past the toilet cleaner, glass cleaner, washing-up liquid and . . . there . . . the rubber gloves. I grab all the packets I can hold in two hands and run.

'It's working,' says Gloria from in among the biscuits. 'I just filled a finger.'

The opening of the gloves is the perfect size; you can hold it tight against your bum cheeks so all the fart is captured inside. I blow out a massive guff and my yellow glove gives a small wave as it begins to fill with gas.

'Got two fingers now,' comes Malc's voice. And then he laughs. 'It looks like my glove is swearing at me.'

'Three fingers,' shouts Gloria.

I blow another trumpet and the glove flaps behind me, swelling with trapped wind.

'Full,' shouts Gloria. 'The glove is full!'

'Seal it,' I shout. 'Then fill another.'

'Full,' shouts the Schnitz. 'How many do we need?'

'As many as we can,' I shout, and with one more mighty toot, my own glove is full of farts from fingers to wrist. I tie it off with an elastic band and start on the next handful of wind.

It's almost three in the morning – and we are exhausted – when we run out of farts. We lay out our work on the floor and count nineteen hands of guff. They bounce lightly on the ground like a crop of very strange fruit.

Next step is to carefully insert lengths of rubber tubing into the opening of the gloves. At one end, the tubes are sealed with corks and at the other they are secured to the gloves with extra-strong sticky tape. It's slow, fiddly work, made even slower and fiddlier because we are all so tired.

But we get it done. We tidy up the shop, gather our fart balloons into three bin-liners and traipse back to our houses. It's after four by the time I get home, pass my fart balloons one by one through Zem's dog flap, and then wriggle in after them. I'm so sleepy I could snooze off on the cold kitchen floor.

In fact I do lie there for a while, and my eyes are just beginning to close when Zem shuffles over to me and licks my face.

'Just let me lie here for five minutes,' I say in a yawny whisper.

Zem yawns too, and I'm so tired it looks like he's talking.

Imagine Dad finding you down here with your feet hanging out of my dog flap, he seems to say. *You'd be in such trouble. Now go bark to bed, quick!* Bark *to bed, get it?*

'Fine,' I say. 'I'm going, just . . . stop talking, you're freaking me out.'

Zem huffs and trots back to his basket.

I drag myself up the stairs and I'm asleep the second my head hits the pillow.

22

TODAY WILL BE MOSTLY SUNNY WITH A HIGH POSSIBILITY OF STRONG WIND.

It feels as if my alarm clock goes off one second after I fall asleep.

I have never felt so tired in my life – it's as if my blanket is holding me onto the bed, as if my eyes have been glued shut and my head filled with cotton wool. Added to that, I have a tummy ache.

It's so, so tempting to hit the snooze button on my alarm but instead I remove my headscarf, slither out from under the world's heaviest blanket and plop onto the floor.

I crawl to the bedroom door, pull myself to my feet

and walk the one hundred miles to the bathroom.

I barely recognise the boy in the bathroom mirror – his eyes are half closed and the skin beneath them is puffy and dark with shadow. Whoever this kid is, he looks as if he's never slept a day in his life.

This calls for a very *very* cold shower.

It's horrible, it's torture, but two minutes under ice-cold water shocks my body awake, and when I check my reflection again my eyes are almost completely open.

Back in my bedroom, I tape the seven fart gloves to my tummy, chest and sides, then pull on my school shirt. I feed the rubber tubes down the sleeves of the shirt – three down the left sleeve, four down the right – and secure them to my wrists with tape. Over this goes my jumper. I don't know if it's my body making up for the cold shower or all of the gubbins taped to my tummy, but I feel uncomfortably hot as I make my way – carefully – downstairs.

'Morning, Bob,' says Dad.

Zem jumps up to say hello, and his paws bounce off the fart-filled gloves stuffed up my jumper. 'Down, boy,' I say firmly. 'Paws on the floor.'

Zem gives me a sideways look, but – big relief – he appears to have given up talking for the time being.

'What you in the mood for?' asks Dad. 'I bought groceries. We've got bread, jam, choco-flakes, eggs, bacon, whatever.'

Bing-bong-a-bing. 'The weather today is mostly sunny with some strong wind and a twenty-two per cent chance of rain.'

'IDA!' shouts Dad. 'Will you just stay out of it, please?'

'Would you like me to order cheese?' asks IDA.

Dad walks over to IDA and covers it with a tea towel. And then another. 'Right, Bob, breakfast?'

At the mention of all that food my tummy tightens.

'Actually, Dad, I'm not hungry.'

'We've got beans,' he says. 'Fancy beans?'

My tummy burbles at the mention of food.

'Honestly, Dad. I'm still full from supper.'

Dad has been bustling about the kitchen and it's only now that he looks at me properly. His eyes go to my tummy.

'You're . . . filling out,' he says.

'Been exercising.'

'Even more reason to have some breakfast.'

'I'm fine. I have to go, I'm meeting Malc.'

'Well, at least take some fruit,' says Dad, shoving a banana into my hand.

I take the banana and leave.

Malc and Gloria are sitting on the front wall outside my house. Gloria with her head resting on Malc's shoulder, both with their eyes closed.

'Morning,' I say.

Neither of them move.

'Guys.'

The Schnitzel lets out a quiet snore.

I shake them gently. 'Guys. Time to, you know, save the world.'

'Gal,' says Gloria. 'I'm a gal.'

'Five more minutes?' says Malc.

'Now,' I say. 'Come on.'

Roaring Gloria and Salty Seadog Schnitzel groan, but they get to their feet and we set off for school, padded out with fart balloons, grumbling with tummy ache and yawning with lack of sleep.

'What's first period?' I ask. 'I'm so tired I can't remember.'

Gloria yawns. 'Food tech.'

'That's good.'

'You like cooking? I didn't know.'

'It's not that, it's just that I don't think I could stay awake if it was maths or physics or history or one of those. At least in cooking we're on our feet.'

'Should make it easier for us to get near Eno too,' says Malc.

'What we cooking?'

'Whatever it is, I hope we don't have to eat it,' says Gloria.

Malc and I groan in agreement.

THE SMELL OF BOILING FRUIT. THE WHIFF OF LAST NIGHT'S GUFFS. THE SUBTLE AROMA OF BURNING EYEBROWS.

We're baking a fruit crumble in teams of three – Gloria is peeling, I'm measuring, Malc is crumbling.

More importantly, the plan appears to be working. Mostly because it's a brilliant plan, but also because there is no school inspector watching our every move. He must be inspecting another class this morning, which makes it easier for us to follow Eno and dust him in trapped farts.

'Your turn,' I say to Gloria.

She sets down a half-peeled apple and walks up

to the table where Eno is baking with Maria Mamooli and Stanley Bennett. Gloria uncorks one of her stink bombs, takes aim and squeezes her elbow against her ribs.

'Oof,' says Stanley. 'Is that you again, Eno?'

'Absolutely not,' snaps Eno. 'As I have already told you fifteen times today, I'm wearing smart trousers.'

'I think maybe they're not working,' says Maria.

'Of course they're working,' says Eno. 'I am a genius, you know.'

Maria holds her nose and waves her hand in front of her face. 'I'm sure you are. It's just that . . . well . . .'

'The smell's definitely coming from you,' says Stanley.

Gloria walks back to the table and we leave Eno, Maria and Stanley to argue it out among themselves.

'I think this must be a first,' says Malc. 'One of our plans actually working.'

'I know,' I say, not quite believing it.

'It's fart-tastic,' says Mac.

'It's trump-mendous,' I add.

'Stink-sational,' says Gloria.

'Don't forget to boil your fruit,' Mr Fahrenheit, the food-tech teacher, shouts. 'We're here to bake, not to make tummies ache.' And he laughs at his little rhyme.

'How many balloons have you got left?' I say.

'All farted out,' says the Schnitz.

'One left,' says Gloria. 'What about you?'

'Three,' I say. 'Three big ones. And I'm going to give Eno all of them all at once. One great big guff to finish him off.'

'Do it,' says Malc.

'I'll need you to hug me,' I say.

'Excuse me?'

'I'll be firing farts out of both arms. I need you to bear-hug me around the middle to squeeze the fart sacks.'

'I'll do it,' says Gloria.

'Nice one,' says Malc.

'But . . .'

But I don't have time to argue, and I suppose we're going to get married one day anyway, so what harm can it do?

Eno has left his table, and for a minute I think he's stormed out of the class or maybe gone for his mid-morning poo, but then I spot him over by the cookers, preparing to boil his apples. This is good; there are five or six other children by the cookers, which means five or six more to witness the failure of his smart trousers.

I get into position as he places his pan of chopped apple onto one of the cooker rings. I uncork the remaining three fart gloves and aim both hands at Eno's bottom. There is a faint whiff of escaping fart gas.

'Ready?' I say to Gloria.

And by way of an answer she wraps her arms around me from behind. I hear someone snigger, but I can't allow myself to be distracted. This is the moment of truth.

Eno turns on the gas under his pan and presses the button, which creates the spark, which ignites the gas.

Eno steps to the side.

Gloria squeezes. Hard.

Three gloves' worth of guff blasts out of the tubes with a drawn-out farting sound and a fantastic stink. The flames beneath Eno's pan flutter in the toxic gust.

I realise our mistake.

But it's too late.

With an ear-ringing *Bang*, the fart gas ignites and explodes, throwing Eno's pan into the air. Water, fruit and pan crash to the floor and I think I can smell singed eyebrows.

Mr Fahrenheit takes in the scene. He looks at the mess on the floor, at Gloria still holding onto my waist and the smoke rising from my eyebrows.

The tingles and the drags happen fast.

Mr Fahrenheit doesn't even have time to say *Detention* before I'm gone – hurled forward through the days and months and years of my future.

STRANGE UNDERPANTS.
RENEWABLE (IF SOMEWHAT SMELLY)
ENERGY.
WIRES IN THE BRAIN.

My ears are still ringing from the explosion and my vision is wobbly, but my surroundings feel familiar. Details leak into my mind as I adjust and settle. The wallpaper, the curtains, the lamp in the corner. I'm home. Or in some future version of it.

Nothing much has changed since I was here this morning but, even so, behind the familiar there is a thick atmosphere – almost thick enough to touch – of strangeness, not normalness, and definitely not rightness.

I notice now that the TV is on. And it's been upgraded

since I last saw it. Although that was roughly twenty-six years ago, so some change is to be expected.

The TV is huge. The size of table-tennis table at least, and almost as big as the wall it's mounted on. It's playing old baby cartoons. Something with a family of pigs.

Behind me a baby chuckles happily and the noise brings me fully into the future.

I turn on the spot to find Future Me sitting on the sofa with Future Gloria beside him. They are smiling. Grinning from ear to ear, actually, but something is wrong with this picture. In fact, a lot is wrong.

The first thing is their pants.

Both Gloria and Future Me are wearing nothing but T-shirts and the most bizarre underpants you can imagine. The pants are made of copper, I think; they're big balloony things, sealed at the waist and thighs with thick rubber gaskets. They look more like old-fashioned diving helmets than underpants.

Future Me laughs at something on the giant TV screen. It's the same babyish burble I heard a moment ago. He claps his hands in delight.

'Hey,' I say. 'What's happening?'

Gloria's eyes swivel towards me. She grins but doesn't answer, and her attention returns to the cartoon.

My stomach tightens and I shiver – a shiver that has nothing to do with the tingles but everything to do with the strangeness of this situation.

Then I notice the pipes. And the tank standing in the corner.

In my own time, we have a boiler in a cupboard upstairs that heats all our hot water. This is an oversized version of that. It's as big as a wardrobe and made of the same copper-coloured metal as the pants and pipes. On the front of the tank is a set of circular dials with needles that seem to indicate how full the thing is.

Connected to the tank are a bunch of black rubber pipes. Some run up through the ceiling. Another snakes through to the kitchen. And two run along the wall and disappear behind the sofa.

When I take a closer look I see that these tubes pass through the back of the sofa and are connected to Future Me and Gloria's strange pants.

Future Me farts and a pipe at the back of the sofa twitches. I follow the line of the pipe back to the tank, where one of the needles wobbles slightly.

'Hello?' I say. 'Anyone?'

It's obvious that something is way off here, and whatever it is it's beginning to seriously freak me out.

'You must be Bob,' says the familiar voice of Si.

The suddenness of it makes me jump.

From the sofa, my future self turns towards me and smiles. 'Bobo,' he says, before returning his attention to the cartoon.

'What happened this time?' I ask.

'*This time*?' says Si. 'An interesting question. The sort of question one might expect from . . . a time traveller.'

'Who said anything about time travel?'

Si laughs robotically. 'How else did you suddenly appear out of thin air?'

'I'm a wild thing,' I say. 'Snuck in through the back door.'

'Not this time,' says Si. 'I detected your arrival.'

And now it's my turn. '*This time?*'

'You have been trying to undo me, Bob. And I don't like that.'

Si is right, of course, but how does it know? How *can* it know?

The way I understand time travel, Si has never seen me before. Every time I travel back to the past I create a new future that erases those that went before. All that stuff with robot gorillas and flying spider droids – I remember it because I lived through it and I carried the memories back through time with me. The only way Si could know about any of that is if someone told it.

'You must be thinking of someone else,' I say. 'I'd

never – Ouch!' I feel a sharp pain just above my ankle. 'What was that?'

'Nothing,' says Si.

I look at the floor just in time to see what looks like a small metallic insect vanish into a panel in the wall. I rub my ankle and my fingers come away with a smear of blood.

'That thing stabbed me!'

'I just took a little blood sample,' says Si, as if he's done nothing more than pinch a hazelnut from my muesli. 'Don't be such a baby.'

'Why would you do that?'

'To check,' says Si.

'Check what?'

'Your DNA. And . . . interesting . . . you really are the same person, aren't you? You and Bob. You really are a time traveller.'

'Er . . .'

'I had my suspicions, but I've never seen it happen

before. We might have to put a stop to that.' Again Si says this calmly and evenly, the way your dad might suggest you need to clean your teeth or brush your hair.

The effect of this simple matter-of-factness is chilling.

'Suspicions. How?'

'You talk a lot,' says Si. 'Or at least you used to.'

I turn to my future self. He giggles idiotically at the TV.

'What have you done?' I say.

'Oh, nothing much,' says Si. 'Just solved the two greatest problems facing humanity.'

'Which are?'

'One: sustainability. Instead of humans draining resources from the planet, humans are now a source of constant renewable energy.'

A fart comes from the direction of the sofa, the pipes rattle and a needle on the huge copper tank moves a little to the right.

'All human gas is now collected and used to create fuel. All heat and electricity is generated from human emissions. And don't look so surprised – you gave me the idea with your funny little fart gloves.'

'You said you've solved two problems. What's the other?'

'Happiness,' says Si.

From the sofa Gloria chuckles at the cartoon.

'Don't they look happy?' says Si.

'They look like . . . like big babies.'

'Adorable, aren't they? And what could be happier than a baby?'

'You've gone insane,' I say. 'Completely and utterly bonkers. What did you do to them?'

'I have hacked into their amygdalae.'

'Their amygwhatnows?'

'I shoved an electric wire into the bit of their brains that creates feelings of pleasure. And the really cool bit is, the electricity comes from the farts. Clever, huh?'

A sound from the kitchen – a squeak – draws my attention.

'What's that?'

'Go and see for yourself,' says Si.

My belly clenches with dread (or it might just be lingering tummy ache from last night's midnight feast), and I follow the sound into the kitchen.

25

ANOTHER ROBOT.
FIGHT OR FLIGHT?
FIGHT!
A VERY SMELLY FLAME THROWER.

Sitting on a high chair at the kitchen table is baby Elvis.

He's not alone.

The robot looming over my son is approximately human in shape: two arms, two legs and a head. The arms and legs are made of exposed pistons, levers and tubing; and the head is roughly the size of a dustbin. Where there should be a face there is a screen, and on the screen a looped video image of Future Gloria's face. The robot holds a yellow plastic spoon in one metal fist; in the other hand it's holding a bowl of mush.

At the sound of me walking into the kitchen, both baby and robot swivel their heads towards me.

Elvis smiles. The image of Gloria does not.

'What have you done to him? Why is he grinning like that? You maniac! Did you shove a wire in my baby's amygdathingummy?'

'The infant is fine,' says Si. 'It's smiling because it's a baby. And it's happy.'

'What's that mush you're feeding him?'

'Banana,' says Si. 'He really likes it.'

'Nananana,' says baby Elvis.

I notice now there is a narrow metal tube attached to the back of his nappy. It seems even baby farts are harvested in this future.

'He should be with his parents,' I say. 'Not a robot.'

'It likes the robot,' says Si. 'The robot never gets tired, is never grumpy, and can sing a selection of over three thousand lullabies with perfect pitch. It can play peek-a-boo for hours without getting bored, it doesn't mind changing nappies and it can imitate the facial expressions of either biological parent. It also does a really cool thing where it makes a penny appear from behind the baby's ear.'

Baby Elvis burbles happily.

'But what about his . . . his future?'

'When the child is eleven we will shove a wire in his brain and his future will be one of uninterrupted happiness.'

'What, farting down a tube and watching cartoons all day?'

'I can tell you're impressed,' says Si.

The problem – one of the many, many problems – with Si, is that it has no body, no presence, no face for me to look into. So I say what I have to say to the robot.

'No,' I say. 'I'm not impressed, I'm . . . disimpressed. I'm the opposite of impressed. This is the worst thing I've seen in my life and I've seen some pretty awful things. It's horrible, and evil and unnatural. You think you're so clever, but you have no idea what it means to be human and you never will.'

I'd hoped my angry rant might bring on the tingles, but – despite everything – I feel somehow calm and not in the least bit tingly. A candle flickers on the kitchen table.

'What's that for?' I ask. 'It's not even dark.'

'It's scented with lavender and chamomile,' says

Si. 'Helps with the fart smell. It's also quite soothing to humans.'

'Nothing about this is soothing!' I shout.

Except the candle is rather relaxing, and I'm nowhere near tingling.

'You will feel differently very soon,' says Si.

'Why? What does that mean?'

'Robot,' says Si, 'take Bob to the living room, connect him to the flatulence tank and insert a junior electrode into his amygdala.'

The robot sets down the spoon and the bowl of mashed bananas. It swivels Gloria's face towards me and takes a step forward.

The floor vibrates under its weight.

'No no no no no. No thank you. No need for that, I'll just . . . you know, go back to where I came from. To the past. And we can forget all about this fart tank and brain wire business.'

'Let you return to the past? So you can try again to

erase me? I think not. Better to keep you here. You'll be happy.'

Yeah, not likely.

'You can't keep me here,' I say. 'Sooner or later Time will take me back to where I belong, and when it does, you'll be sorry.'

'I don't think so,' says Si. 'The amygdala controls our "fight or flight" response. Do you know what that is?'

'It might have been mentioned in biology,' I say.

'Well, it's my theory – because I am super intelligent, remember – that you possess some kind of anomaly in your amygdala, which has enhanced your fight or flight response to the extent that you can move through time.'

'I got about half of that,' I say. 'Run it by me again.'

Si laughs. 'You're playing for time, Bob, but I'm afraid your time has run out. Robot, grab the child.'

The giant robot may have been built by a super-intelligent computer program, but it's never played tag on the playground. So when the robot lumbers towards me, I fake one way then dodge the other, running round to the opposite side of the kitchen table.

Baby Elvis claps.

The robot swivels around at the waist and comes back for me. This time I duck under the table and pop up on the side closest to the kitchen door.

Stupid robot.

The robot raises both fists above its head and smashes them down onto the kitchen table, reducing it to seven billion splinters, a cloud of dust and a smouldering scented candle. Some of the larger splinters catch light, and they flicker like struck matches.

The video image of Gloria's face roars in anger.

Elvis bursts into tears.

'Stop this now!' shouts Si, and all pretence of being calm and reasonable has vanished.

I run for the kitchen door, but it's locked and the key is nowhere to be seen.

The floor vibrates under the robot's heavy steps,

Elvis wails and Si – Si is laughing.

I slam my shoulder into the door but it doesn't budge and now my shoulder hurts. I try kicking it, but instead of slamming into wood, my shoe hits something else, there is a clattering sound and my foot is suddenly on the other side of the door.

It can't be.

After all these years and with all this technology, Zem's dog flap is still in place. If I'd seen it a moment ago I might have made it through to the other side, but now my foot is stuck and the robot is steadily closing in. I yank my foot free, giving my shin a nasty scrape in the process.

As the robot reaches for me, I duck under its arm and run back towards the living room, where I might be able to escape through a window. The robot swivels quickly, reaches out a long metal arm and catches hold of the sleeve of my jumper.

I keep running and my jumper sleeve stretches to

twice its length before tearing free. Suddenly released from the robot's grip, I shoot forward, my feet slipping on the wreckage of the kitchen table. I fall flat onto my front and knock all the wind out of my tummy. More than that, I land on the fart balloons taped to my body and the impact pops all seven corks from their tubes. The sound is like gunfire.

Elvis claps in delight. 'Popopopop.'

There must have been traces of fart left in each of the balloons and the fall squeezes it all from the gloves. The gas blasts over the smouldering wreckage of the table and two or three pieces of wood take flame.

The smell is awful, and now, finally here come the tingles.

But I can't afford to wait. I get to my feet, grab a burning table leg and hold it in front of me. The robot takes a step forward. It isn't scared of a little fire.

A thought:

But what about a lot *of fire?*

I run for the living room, where my future self and future wife are still laughing and drooling at the TV. The robot follows me into the room and I climb up and over the sofa so my back is against the wall.

I glance towards the window.

'And now you're trapped.' Si laughs. 'It's reinforced glass, Bob. You'd have more luck jumping through a brick wall. Now, put down the wood before you cause a fire. And then we can get this over with.'

'Yes, let's,' I say.

I look down at the back of the sofa, at the two rubber tubes collecting farts from Future Me and Gloria. I also notice – with considerable disappointment – that Future Me still has a bald patch, despite me sleeping in a silk headscarf for the past two nights. But no time to dwell . . .

I raise my right foot and stamp it down on one of the fart tubes. It comes away on the second stamp and starts to hiss. The fart tank rattles, the needles on the dials move backwards and a stream of stinking fart gas billows up from the open end of the tube.

'Stop that!' shouts Si. 'Stop it now!'

I snatch up the rubber tube and aim it at the Robot.

'Put it down!' screams Si.

I hold the burning table leg in front of the giant fart tube. There is a loud *WHOOoomPH!* and a column of blueish fire shoots from the end of the tube. The flame hits the robot directly in the chest and the image of Gloria's face flickers and screams and glitches.

Si screams. No words, just a loud and terrifying scream.

Water sprinkles down from the ceiling but the drags have me now – my legs are jelly and my arms elastic, but I hold onto my fart flame thrower and continue to blast the robot. It swivels at the waist and its arms flail wildly in the air. I feel kind of bad for it, but then it was about to shove a wire in my amygdawhachamacallit so I don't feel *too* bad.

'Robot!' shouts Si. 'Do something.'

The drags are heavy now.

The last thing I see is the robot staggering backwards into the giant TV and falling to the ground in a cloud of sparks.

And then . . .

. . . I'm gone.

26

BOILING FRUIT. AGAIN.
THE SCHOOL INSPECTOR LOSES HIS BREAKFAST.
DETENTION AGAIN. AGAIN.

I can still smell the ghost of all that guff when I find myself back in Mr Fahrenheit's food-tech class. I blow out through my nose to clear the memory of the awful smell.

'You OK?' asks Malc.

To look at me you wouldn't know I'd just narrowly escaped having my brain rewired by a massive bin-headed robot. Time has reset itself – my jumper is unstretched, I'm free of dust and splinters, and my remaining fart gloves are inflated and full of guff.

(My leg still hurts though, from kicking my foot through Zem's dog flap, and I'd bet I have a wicked scrape up my shin. Time can be awkward like that.)

'Your turn, Bob,' says Gloria.

'Turn?'

She nods at Eno, who is carrying a pan of apples over to the cookers. 'The farts,' she says. 'It's your turn.'

'I can't. We have to stop before it's too late. If it isn't already too late.'

'What?' She looks around. 'Is the inspector here?'

I shake my head.

'Don't forget to boil your fruit,' shouts Mr Fahrenheit.

'We're here to bake,' I say, a split second before the teacher says the same thing. 'Not to make tummies ache.'

Malcolm's mouth drops open. 'It's true. You do time travel.'

I nod. 'It's true. And trust me, we need to abandon the plan.'

'You mean to say we broke into Dad's shop for nothing?' says Malc.

'It was kind of fun,' says Gloria, yawning.

Actually, it was kind of a gigantic flaming disaster, I think. The remaining fart gloves feel like unexploded bombs beneath my clothes and I have a sudden and desperate urge to be rid of them. If they were to go off by accident, who knows what damage I might cause to the future?

'Sir,' I say, holding my hand up.

'Bob?'

'Need to go to the toilet, sir.'

Mr F nods. 'Be quick. And don't forget to wash your hands.'

Once out of the classroom, I run down the corridor towards the loos. The corridor turns left and – *why not?* – I slide across the polished floor as I approach the turn. It's a good skid, taking me almost all the way to the bend. When the skid fades, I continue running, flying around the turn and crashing smack into the school inspector.

We both tumble to the floor, the inspector landing on his bum and me landing on three fart gloves. The guff blasts directly into the inspector's face. He retches, turns his head to the side, almost vomits, appears to get himself under control, and then vomits anyway.

I can't be one hundred per cent certain, but it looks like he might have had porridge for breakfast.

A shadow falls over us and I turn my head to see a looming Mr McUnger, bucket at his feet, mop in his hand. Looking up at him feels – I imagine – like it must have felt in the olden days, staring up at an executioner.

McUnger makes a low growling sound. It's a three-syllable growl, and I'm reasonably certain those syllables translate into a single word: *Detention.*

ONE OF THOSE SIT-DOWN TELLINGS-OFF. IDA GETS RECYCLED. I GET THE MESSY DRAWER.

'What's going on?'

This is one of those sit-down tellings-off. The ones that are conducted like an interview or an interrogation. Where they make you sit at the table and 'explain yourself'.

I prefer the ones where they just send you to your room. Or tell you they're 'disappointed'. Or just shout. I can handle those. But these sit-downs are the worst.

Dad drums his fingers on the kitchen table. Waiting for an answer.

I shrug.

Dad bangs the palm of his hand on the table, making me jump.

'Bob! This is serious. Do you understand me?'

Zem, who was curled up at my feet, makes an apologetic grumble, gets up and heads off towards the garden.

'Well?' says Dad.

I nod. Then quickly add, 'Yes. I understand.'

'Do you though? Because this is the third time we've had this conversation this week. Three times you've acted up in school. Three times you've been given detention. And when I ask for an explanation, all you have to say for yourself is . . . a shrug?'

I've never seen Dad get this worked up before, and I'm so nervous I very nearly shrug again. Instead I mutter something that even I can't understand. It's a kind of vowel-and-consonant soup that resembles words but means nothing.

Dad takes a deep breath. I feel bad for him. I mean, if my son came home with a note saying he'd made a school inspector vomit, I suppose I'd be pretty angry too.

'What I don't understand,' says Dad, 'one of the *many* things I don't understand, is why you thought it would be a good idea to turn yourself – and your friends – into some sort of . . . human fart machine.'

To save the world, Dad.

Except I didn't. I just made it worse.

'And you know the worst thing about it?' says Dad.

'Making the school inspector puke?'

'No,' says Dad. 'Although that was pretty awful. The worst thing is, it was kind of brilliant.'

'Brilliant?'

'It was ingenious,' says Dad. 'Silly, pointless, disgusting. But as silly pointless disgusting things go, it was very . . . inventive.'

I smile.

Dad doesn't, so I let the smile slide.

'I say this because you clearly have a good – if slightly odd – head on your shoulders. If you applied yourself to something constructive, who knows what you might achieve. But this . . . all this nonsense with insects and eggs and farts – it has to stop, Bob.'

I nod.

'Is it . . . am I . . . am I not giving you enough attention? If I'm not, you have to tell me.'

'No. It's not you. It's . . .' There are times when only a shrug will do. This is one of them.

'I dunno what we're going to do with you,' Dad says. 'I just have no idea.'

Bing-bong-a-bing! 'IDA is here. How can I help you?'

Dad slams his hand on the table. 'I said *I have no idea*, not IDA!'

'IDA knows lots of things,' says IDA. 'Why not ask me a question?'

'Can you just stay out of it?'

'No need to be rude,' says IDA.

Dad glares at the machine. He gets up from the table, unplugs IDA and drops it into the bin. 'Should have done that a long time ago.'

There is a small circle in the dust on top of the kitchen counter where IDA used to stand. Listening to everything we say.

And suddenly, it all makes sense. When I asked Si how it knew about my plans, it said that I talk a lot. I thought it meant Future Me, but it meant the me in the here and now. Because what IDA hears today (IDA plus all our smart phones and watches and doorbells and everything else) Si knows tomorrow.

Which means whatever I do next (and I have no idea whatsoever what that might be) I'll have to keep it quiet. Otherwise, who knows what it might inspire Si to do.

Dad sits back down at the table.

'Bob,' he says. 'Son. Is this – all this mucking about

and acting up – is it about Mum?'

And that could mean one of two things.

It could mean: *Are you acting like an imbecile because you don't know how to handle the grief and pain of losing your mother less than a year ago?*

Or, maybe Dad knew Mum was a time traveller and what he's saying is: *Son, your mother was a time traveller. It caused a few odd moments but we got through them. Together. If it's happening to you, tell me and we'll work it out. Together.*

I fidget in my seat.

'You can tell me,' Dad says.

One thing I am not going to do is use my mother's death as an excuse.

So if I answer yes to Dad's question, then I will have to tell him everything. Including the fact that the future human race has been enslaved by a cruel super-intelligence.

It also means telling him I'm married. And that

my wife has had a baby.

And talk about *embarrassing*.

Dad reaches across the table and places his hand gently on top of mine. 'Want to tell me about it?'

Real answer: Yes.

Also real answer: No.

What comes out of my mouth: 'Maybe.'

Dad nods like he understands, and maybe he does. 'When you're ready,' he says. 'But . . .' He makes a gesture with his hands as if to take in me and everything I've done this past couple of days, 'don't leave it too long. OK?'

'OK.'

Dad gets up from the table. 'Right,' he says. 'I'll cook supper, and you . . .' he thinks, 'you can clean up the messy drawer.'

'But, Dad!'

'Messy drawer. Now.'

28

PENCILS, PINS AND PAPER CUTS.
SO THAT'S WHAT WAS WRONG WITH MY
WALKIE.
CODEWORD: PIRATES.
ANYTHING'S POSSIBLE.

You know the one.

The drawer where you shove all the random stuff that has no obvious place of its own. Pens, pencils, scissors, rolls of tape, receipts, scribbled notes, keys, buttons, envelopes, screws and nails, needles and pins, little metal tools, shoelaces, combs and brushes, elastic bands, batteries old and new, tissues, gum, old credit cards, toothpicks, marbles, ping-pong balls, clips, corks, mystery bits of wood and plastic that look like they might be important, rubbers, dust and crumbs, ointment, glue and a pot of glitter (which will come in handy when I finally get round to making Dad's Father's Day card), plugs, leads, tea bags, ribbon, pots without lids and lids without pots, straws, matches, hooks, brushes, a penknife, the handle off a mug and plenty of string.

I think cleaning and sorting the messy drawer is even worse than picking up dog poo or dusting cobwebs. It's messy, sticky, frustrating and boring work. I have been stabbed by pins and I have a paper cut.

And all the time, I couldn't stop thinking about how I'm going to save the world.

Dad said I'm ingenious, which I'm pretty sure is a good thing – maybe not as impressive as a *genius* genius, but certainly better than a complete and utter fool. Even so, I'm all out of ideas and I feel like a failure. I have a baby in the future, and if I don't do something, he could live his life wearing an electric collar, eating nanobot cake, or hooked up to a massive fart tank.

If I don't do something, little Elvis will never feel grass between his toes or snow down the back of his jumper. He will never ride a bike non-handed, spin on a roundabout until he's dizzy or eat a crisp-and-mayonnaise sandwich.

I can't let this be my child's future. I can't give up.

One upside of cleaning out the messy drawer is that I found two reasonably healthy-looking batteries. And two is all I need. I take the back off my walkie – which looks more bashed-up than I remember – and replace the dead batteries with the new.

I turn it on and a green light flickers, fades, thinks about dying and then glows as brightly as it ever has. I push the talk button.

'Malc?'

The walkie crackles but there's no answer.

I push the button again and a tickle of electricity fizzes across the backs of my fingers.

'Malc? Can you hear me? Over.'

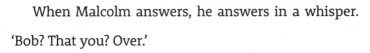

The handset crackles, and another fizz of electricity tickles my hand.

When Malcolm answers, he answers in a whisper. 'Bob? That you? Over.'

His voice sounds funny. Kind of rough. Maybe taking the walkie in and out of the future has damaged it.

'Who else would it be? Over.'

'It's good to hear your voice, old friend. Over.'

Old friend?

'Er, yeah, you too. Over.'

'Where are you calling from? Over.'

'Home of course. Over.'

'What about Si?' says the Schnitz. 'Over.'

'You mean the school inspector? Well, Dad made me clean out the messy drawer, but that's all. Over.'

'Messy drawer? School inspector? What are you on

about, Bob? Did Si mess with your brain or something? Over.'

'Almost,' I say. 'But not quite. Over.'

'Are you sure? Your voice sounds funny. Over.'

'Funny how? Over.'

'High and wobbly,' says Malcolm. 'Like you're a little boy again. Over.'

'I am a little boy. Well, not *that* little. Over.'

'Very funny. Over.'

'It wasn't meant to be. And now that you mention it, you sound like an old man. Over.'

'Ouch. Thirty-seven's not that old. Over.'

Wait.

What?

'You still there?' Malc says. 'Over.'

A thought . . .

'What year is it? Over.'

Malc laughs. A deep, throaty, grown-up laugh. 'Are you sure you're OK? Over.'

'The year, Malc. What's the year? Over.'

'2049,' he says. 'Over.'

I look at the walkie in my hand. At the scrapes and scratches that weren't there two days ago. And, now that I'm examining it more closely, I see the colour has faded too, the bright red washed out to more of a bubble-gum pink. This walkie looks old.

Wait.

This walkie *is* old. I must have picked up my *future* walkie-talkie that time the gorilla attacked me, right before I jumped into the rosebush.

I guess the big question is: *What is it connected to?*

'Give me a second,' I say into the handset. 'Over.'

I run to my bedroom window and pull it open. 'Malc!'

The Schnitzel's window opens and he pops his head out. 'What is it?'

'What are you doing?' I say. 'Right now.'

'Talking to you.'

'No. Just before that.'

'Oh, pulling faces in the mirror. Seeing if I could scare myself.'

'You weren't on your walkie?'

'Of course not. You said your batteries were flat.'

'Right. Good. Cool.'

'You OK?' says Malc.

'I think so. I'll explain later.'

The Schnitz disappears back into his bedroom and I pick up the faded and bashed walkie-talkie.

'Hello. Over.'

'Bob?' says the voice of what can only be Future Malcolm. 'What's this all about? Over.'

'Do you remember when I used to talk about being a time traveller? Over.'

'I don't know who you are, but I'm ending this call,' says Future Malc. 'Over and ou—'

'Wait! Malc, wait. I can prove it. Over.'

Or at least I think *I can.*

The line is silent and I think I've lost him. Then: 'How? Over.'

'You know the place where you leave notes for me? In the year 2049? Over.'

'Yes, the g—'

'Don't tell me. But I do need you to pick a code word. Over.'

'A what? Over.'

'Just pick a word, Malc. Over.'

'OK, my code word is . . . *pirates*. Over.'

'Good one. Now, go to the place where we swap notes. I'm going to write the code word on a piece of paper and leave it there. If you find it, then you'll know I am who I say I am. Over.'

'But you haven't done it yet. Over.'

'No, but I will. Take your walkie and call me when you find the note. Over.'

'How do I know this isn't a trap? Over.'

'Because you never told me where you drop the

notes. That's something only your best friend would know. Over.'

Malc answers straight away: 'I'll be there in ten minutes. Over and out.'

When I told Dad I wanted to take Zem for a walk, he offered to come with me. But I told him I wanted to be alone, that I wanted to visit Mum's grave, and Dad said fine. He also said that if I got up to any more nonsense, he would ground me for the rest of my life. Which is kind of funny considering that's exactly what's in store, not just for me but for the whole world, if I can't find a way to stop Si.

Before I left, I scribbled the code word on a scrap of paper and – because it's not going to be found for almost thirty years – placed the paper inside a plastic bag. And then I placed that inside another plastic bag.

The graveyard is quiet at this time of night, so I let Zem off the lead to run and sniff among the gravestones. So long as he doesn't start digging, there shouldn't be any problem.

Mum's flowers sit in a small pot buried in the ground so that the opening is level with the top of the soil. I hide the code-word package beneath the pot, take a seat on the bench and wait for Time to do its thing.

In the distance a clock bongs the hour and I shudder. Annoyingly, it's seven o'clock in the evening, so there are another six bongs to go before the awful sound is over with.

It's not that this clock makes a particularly harsh sound, it's just a thing I have with big clocks.

Mum, you see, was killed by one.

And yes, I know how ridiculous that sounds.

The clock in question was as wide across as a kitchen table and made from steel and glass. According to the newspaper report, it weighed over one tonne. It had been hanging above the bank for eighty-three years. That's more than thirty thousand days.

Over seven hundred thousand hours. Upwards of four million minutes of tick-tick-ticking without once coming loose. Then it picked the exact second my mother was walking beneath it to fall free of its old and rusted brackets.

Have you ever seen one of those films where someone dies a ridiculous death? They get flattened by a falling piano, sat on by an elephant, drowned in custard. I always wondered how it was for the family of the strangely departed. Would they laugh at the funeral?

From experience, as the son of a mother who was killed by an enormous falling clock, I can say with a reasonable degree of certainty that they would not. (I suppose the exception might be the one where someone is flattened by an elephant. I imagine the coffin would be very wide and incredibly thin. I mean, how could you not laugh at that?)

At least they didn't put it on her gravestone:

The clock struck one then struck my mum.

If it sounds like I'm being disrespectful, please believe I'm not. It's just . . . it's a hard thing to come to terms with, is all.

At least the clock has stopped bonging now.

And then, in the silence, my walkie crackles.

'Is this some kind of trick?' says Future Malc. 'Over.'

'You found it then? It worked? Over.'

'So you really are a time traveller. Over.'

'Yep. And now you're going to help me save the world. Over.'

'Does that mean I can stop living in the forest? Over.'

'That's the plan. Your best friend misses you. Over.'

'I miss him too. And being warm at night, and eating food that isn't covered in soil. So tell me everything you've done so far. Don't leave anything out. Over.'

I tell him.

Malc laughs. 'The fart gloves sound brilliant,' he says. 'But you –' he laughs again – 'you thought you could destroy Eno's smart trousers with *ants*? Over.'

'We got a bit carried away with the bugs idea. Over.'

'A bug is a fault in something's software. It's accidental. A virus is a piece of code written deliberately to mess up a computer program. It spreads from one device to another, which is why it's called a virus. Understand? Over.'

'A bit. I'm not very good at computers. Over.'

'I wasn't either. Until I started teaching myself to code during the "Big Stink". Over.'

'I heard. Future Me said you mucked about with our smart pants. Over.'

'Yeah, I wrote a never-ending fart-laugh loop. Completely ruined them. Over.'

Future Malc laughs. And then stops abruptly.

We speak at the same time:

'The fart-laugh loop. Over.'

'Do you think you could recreate it?' I say. 'Over.'

'I'm sure I can. But how do we get the virus into his pants? Over.'

'Eno said his pants can connect to anything. Do you think that includes walkie-talkies? Over.'

'You'd have to get pretty close to him. Like, arm's-length close. And you'd have to stay there for a while. Over.'

'How long? Over.'

'Hard to say. Two minutes? Three? Maybe as many as five. Over.'

'But do you think it will work? Over.'

'I think if we can walkie-talkie through time, then anything's possible. Over.'

'OK, you get working on the code. I'll figure out a way of getting close to Eno. Over and out.'

I sit for a while longer in the graveyard, thinking – hoping – that Mum might show up. But after twenty minutes I'm still alone and Zem is getting restless. Maybe Mum talking to me here was a one-off. Or maybe she never came at all and I imagined the whole thing.

* * *

Back at home, I open my bedroom window and whisper-shout into the night: *'Breakfast meeting at eight o'clock.'*

Malc's voice comes back on the breeze: 'See you there.'

Gloria answers by knocking three times on my bedroom wall.

RETURN OF THE FART-LAUGH LOOP.
GETTING CLOSE TO ENO.
A FLUSH OF INSPIRATION.
'THIS PLAN STINKS.'

Malc and Gloria arrive bang on time. Schnitz is wearing a black headscarf printed with tiny white stars and eating a bowl of cornflakes. Gloria is holding a plate of beans on toast.

'Want some?' Gloria asks, holding out her plate.

I pick up a small square of soggy toast, pop it into my mouth and mutter a thank you.

'So,' says Gloria, 'I assume we're –'

I hold a finger to my lips. 'Shhh!'

'Rude,' says Gloria.

'Wait,' I say. And I hold up a sign I made last night.

Written on a piece of white paper are the words: *The smart devices are all listening.*

And, because I was enjoying myself, I decorated it with a picture of a robot and some swirls.

'Cool robot,' says Malc.

I hold up another card and aim it at Gloria: *Turn your smart watch off.*

Gloria pulls a face. 'I'm counting my steps.'

Another card. This one shows another robot – a giant version of the one that tried to pull my arm off on my last jaunt – holding a tiny human in each of its shining metal fists. Written above the robot are the words: *Or else!!!*

'Fine,' says Gloria. She puts her breakfast down, removes her watch and turns it off. 'Happy now?'

'Getting there,' I say. 'Now, pay attention.'

And while my friends eat their breakfasts, I tell them about last night's conversation with Future Malcolm. I tell them about bugs and viruses, about the fart-laugh loop, and how it is going to save the world.

'So,' I say, 'everything clear?'

They both have their mouths full of breakfast so it takes a moment for them to answer.

'You spoke to Future Me?' Malc asks.

'Yep.'

'How did he sound?'

'Like you but more grown-up.'

The Schnitzel thinks about this and nods as if the answer has satisfied him. 'Can I speak to him?'

'Best not to,' I say. 'You might mess up your future. Plus, we need to save the batteries.'

'Why do you never speak to Future Me?' Gloria asks.

'Er . . .'

I do. And we're married. And we've had a baby called Elvis.

I feel my face turning red.

'Wait,' Gloria says, suddenly alarmed. 'I'm not dead, am I? Or in jail? Or dead in jail?'

'Not dead,' I say. 'Not in jail. Now, can we all just concentrate for five minutes on saving the world?'

Gloria gestures for me to carry on.

'Future Malc is working on the code,' I say. 'All we need to do is come up with a plan to get close and stay close to Eno for maybe five minutes.'

'How close?' asks Gloria.

I hold my hands an arm's length apart.

'Eew,' says Gloria.

'I know. Also, he can't know what we're up to.'

'Why not?'

'Because then he'll know we hacked his pants and just go and make a new pair. He needs to think they malfunctioned all on their own. That it's a *bug*. Then he'll go home, hook them up to his computer and the *virus* will spread, ruining his pants and his code for good. So . . . any ideas?'

'I could wrestle him,' Malc says. 'Then, while I'm sitting on him, you do the walkie stuff.'

'It might work,' I say. 'But we'd probably get separated by a teacher. And even if we didn't, he'll be struggling. If the connection between the pants and walkie is broken for even a second, then the whole thing fails.'

'I'll dance with him,' says Gloria. 'I'll do my cha-cha-cha.'

'I don't think Eno's much of a dancer,' I say. 'And besides, how would you hold the walkie if you're holding Eno?'

The garage is at the back of the house, joined onto the side of the downstairs loo, and from inside the house comes the sound of the toilet flushing.

'We're running out of time,' I say. 'It's eight fifteen already.'

'How'd you do that?' says Gloria.

'What?'

'Tell the time without looking at your watch.'

'Dad's very regular.'

'Regular?'

'Well, unless Zem has learned to use the toilet – which would be awesome – that was Dad, having his ten-past-eight poo. The flush goes at eight fifteen, regular as clockwork.'

There's an idea in the air and we all feel it. You can tell by the expression on Malcolm and Gloria's faces – it's that look you have when a word slips out of your brain and you're struggling to grab hold of it. We all sense that the answer to our problem is right before us, waiting for one of us to catch up and take hold of it.

Gloria gets there first.

'Eno's mid-morning poo,' she says.

'Yes,' says Malc. 'Eleven twenty, just before the end of first break.'

'Regular as clockwork,' I say. 'He'll be sitting still, and because he's inside a cubicle he won't see us with the walkie. It's got to work!'

'So we follow him into the toilet?' says Gloria. 'While he does his whatnots? Gross.'

'You can wait outside, stick an "out of order" sign on the door and stop anyone else from coming in after Eno.'

'OK,' says Gloria. 'But what if Mr McUnger turns up? He scares me.'

'He scares everyone,' I say. 'Maybe tell him Mrs Plink wants to see him in her office. Cry. Throw yourself on the floor. You'll think of something.'

'Excellent,' says Gloria, looking quite excited at the idea.

'This is what we'll do: Eno goes into one of the cubicles and sits down to do what has to be done. I'll go into the next cubicle and hold the walkie close to the wall while the other Malc – Future Malc – does all the clever stuff.'

'What do I do?' asks the Schnitzel.

'Stand outside the cubicle in case he finishes early. We have to keep him in the lavvy for at least five minutes.'

'How am I supposed to do that?'

'Lean on it. Count yourself lucky you're not me, I'm going to be right next to the action.'

'This plan stinks,' says Malc.

'Yes,' I say. 'It does, but it's the only one we've got.'

A CLOSE-UP VIEW OF UNDIES.
THIS PLAN REALLY DOES STINK.
A SCUFFLE IN THE CUBICLES.

We are all in place by eleven fifteen.

Gloria is waiting in the corridor, ready to tape a sign to the door as soon as Eno comes in.

Inside, there are four toilet cubicles – Malc is hiding in number one and I'm in number three. Eno, when he arrives, will have two choices – stall number two or stall number four. Either way, I'll be right next door. As soon as Eno takes his seat, Malc will exit stall one and take up position outside Eno's chosen place of business.

'What time is it?' whispers the Schnitz.

I look my watch. 'He'll be here any moment.'

I turn on the walkie and press the button. 'Malc, are you there? Over.'

'Here. Over,' says Future Malc down the handset.

'Here,' says the other Malc in cubicle one.

'Not you.'

'Who?' say both Malcs at the same time.

I take my thumb off the walkie-talkie button. 'I'm talking to Future You,' I say to Malc. 'You just sit tight and stay schtum.'

'What's schtum?'

'Quiet. It just sounds cooler.'

'OK. Schtum. Gotcha.'

The door to the toilets opens and I hear shoes on the tiled floor.

I push the talk button on the walkie and drop my voice to a whisper. 'He's here. Over.'

'OK,' whispers Future Malc. 'Hold the walkie as close as possible to the trousers and keep listening. Over.'

'Understood. Over.'

There is a moment of silence and then Eno enters the stall to my left – number four. I hear him lift the toilet lid, unzip his trousers and sit down. A second later, I hear the Schnitzel exit stall number one, hear his footsteps, see his shadow pass in front of my stall and then he comes to a stop outside Eno's poo cabin.

Everything is quiet.

I hold the walkie to the cubicle door and hold my ear to the walkie. My head, in other words, is very close to Eno and what Eno is doing. Eno makes a sound that's part grumble part groan. It's the sound of effort and I try not to think too much about it.

'Can you get any closer?' says Future Malc. 'Over.'

'What's that?' says Eno. 'Did somebody say something?'

I make a toilety grunt by way of an answer.

'Charming,' says Eno.

The cubicle walls and door don't go all the way to the ground. There is a gap – just about big enough for a snake, a cat, a rat, a hedgehog or maybe – at a squeeze – a small dog to fit through. This has always bothered me – the possibility of an animal invading my cubicle and attacking me – but today it gives me a clear view of Eno's feet and his smart trousers, puddled around his ankles. Also, I now know that Eno wears Peppa Pig undies.

'Get closer,' Future Malc says into my ear. 'Over.'

There's only one thing for it, I get down on my hands and knees and press the walkie to the very bottom of the wall, just above the gap. The floor is wet, and I really hope it's because Mr McUnger has just mopped in here, and not because someone with a full bladder and terrible aim recently paid a visit. There's no way to be sure, but it certainly doesn't smell like soapy water.

'In position,' I whisper into the walkie.

'Good work,' says Future Malc. 'We're connected. Over.'

'Who's there?' says Eno.

'Mind your own business,' I say out loud.

'Trebor? Is that you?'

'Do you mind?' I say. 'I'm not really in a chatty mood.'

'Then why are you muttering?'

'Listen,' I say. 'You do your thing your way. I'll do mine mine.'

'Well, your muttering is putting me off, Trebor.'

Good! The longer I can keep him here the better.

Eno starts whistling. He's pretty good.

'You always whistle on the loo?' I say.

'Only when I have to drown out your muttering.' And he continues whistling even louder.

I sit for a while, walkie pressed to the wall, listening and waiting. I'm beginning to worry that maybe Future Malc has gone, that the walkie has failed, or that Time has realised it's made a big mistake and decided to put a stop to all this.

It's making me nervous and I push the talk button on the handset.

'How long to go?' I say. 'Over.'

'None of your business,' says Eno. 'And why do you keep saying "over"?'

'Ouch!'

'What?' says Eno. 'What happened?'

The walkie gave me a small shock is what happened.

'Nothing,' I say.

'You should eat more fibre,' says Eno. And he resumes his whistling.

'Malc,' I whisper into the walkie. 'Are you still there? Over.'

There is a splashing sound in the next cubicle and I catch a whiff of something extremely unpleasant. I pinch my nose with my free hand.

'How dong dow? Over.'

'Dong dow? Over.'

I release my nose. 'How long now? Over.'

'Minutes,' says Future Malc. 'Maybe two. Over.'

The sound of a flushing toilet thunders through the wall between Eno's cubicle and mine. I guess the tummy massager in his smart pants really does get things moving. From next door comes the slide and click of Eno unlocking his cubicle door.

I hold my breath.

Not just because of the smell – although it is awful – but because the future of the world now depends on Malc – little Malc – being able to keep Eno in his cubicle for the next two minutes.

The door rattles in Eno's cubicle. 'Door's stuck,' says Eno. And then there's a bang as he hammers his fists against it. 'Hello,' says Eno, rattling the door on its hinges. 'Hello?'

But the door – and Malcolm – hold.

The walkie fizzes in my hand.

'Still there?' I say into the handset. 'Over.'

'Of course I'm still here,' says Eno. 'Someone is blocking my door. Who is that?' He hammers on the door. 'Let me out!'

I see Eno's feet beneath the door. He takes two steps back then charges forward. *Bdump!*

'Malc,' I say into the walkie. 'How long? Over.'

'Under a minute. If the walkies hold. They're not built for this. Over.'

Eno takes another two steps away from the door and charges again. *Bdump.*

'Bob,' says Malc from outside, 'I can't hold it much longer.'

'Schnitzel,' says Eno. 'I might have guessed.'

From Eno's cubicle comes the biggest bang yet – *Bddddumpp* – and it's a wonder the thing is still standing.

'Bob!' shouts Malcolm. 'I can't hold it.'

I watch Eno's feet take two steps back. He twists his feet on the tiles as if getting a good grip. He begins counting backwards: 'Five . . . four . . .'

I have to keep him in the cubicle. The world depends on it. So I lie flat on the wet floor, reach under the gap with my free hand and grab Eno by the ankle.

Eno screams. He kicks and wriggles but I am holding on with everything I have.

'Let go!' shouts Eno. 'You . . . you . . . lunatic. Ha! Lunatic. Get it? Loo-natic.'

And then, with his other foot, he kicks me in the hand. It hurts, a lot, but I manage to keep my grip on his ankle.

In my other hand, the walkie crackles and hisses. It's almost too hot to hold and I can smell burning.

'Almost done,' says Future Malc. 'Maybe ten more seconds. It's been nice meeting you. Over.'

Under the toilet wall gap, Eno is now using his hands to prise my fingers off his ankle. He uncurls my little finger first, then moves on to the next.

Future Malc's voice is growing faint, the connection is thick with static and I can't make out all of his words: 'I don't thin— take much m— just – more seconds – Over.'

Eno removes my middle finger from his ankle and I'm holding on with nothing more than one finger, one thumb and pure determination.

'You're breaking up,' says Future Malc. 'Over.'

There is a loud bang. Smoke pours from the mouthpiece of the walkie and the heat is too much. I drop the handset to the floor where it fizzes and hisses on the wet tiles. Eno frees his ankle from my grasp. He storms out of the cubicle and – with a massive slam of the door – the bathroom. He doesn't even wash his hands.

In the few seconds it takes me get off the floor and out of the loos, Eno is long gone.

'How'd it go?' asks Gloria. 'Sounded like chaos.'

I shake my head. 'Don't know.'

'It was frantic,' says Malcolm. 'Totally frantic.'

'Lucky,' says Gloria, looking a little disappointed. 'No one bothered me at all.'

31

IF YOU TRAVELLED INTO THE FUTURE, WHAT WOULD YOU SEE? WHAT WOULD YOU BE? FRRRRRRTTTTT!!!

First lesson after break is English with Mr Redrum. We're doing a 'big write' – three pages on the subject of 'When I grow up I want to be . . .'

Heads are bent over notebooks. Pens scribble. But the connection broke on the walkie before Future Malc had a chance to say if he'd succeeded in transmitting the virus to Eno's trousers. My classmates are writing pages on being doctors and train drivers and celebrity bakers, but for all I know every single one of them could grow up connected to a fart tank.

While Mr Redrum sits behind his desk, the inspector walks between the desks. He passes Eno's desk, glances at his work and then moves on.

Eno turns round in his seat and whispers, 'You stink, Trebor.'

'You stink,' I whisper back.

Not the cleverest of comebacks, I agree. Particularly because I really do stink. Dad is going to freak when he sees the state of my school uniform. Again.

And as well as everything else, all that rolling around on the wet floor has made the felt pen run on my school trousers.

Mr Yates stops beside my desk and glances at the blank page in my workbook.

'Nothing, Trebor?'

'Sir.'

'You don't want to be stunt man when you grow up? All that diving over volcanoes, hmm?'

Someone sniggers.

'Maybe you could work with insects, no?'

Another chuckle.

'Or perhaps something to do with gas and tubes. A plumber, perhaps?'

'Don't know, sir.'

Mr Yates squats down so that our eyes are level. A quick smile bends his lips. 'If you could click your fingers and travel thirty years into the future, what would you see there? What would you be?'

I almost laugh.

'I'd like to be a . . .'

'Yes?'

'A good dad, sir.'

Eno snorts.

Mr Yates frowns, as if trying to decide whether I'm being serious or cheeky. And then he nods and stands up. 'Very good,' he says. 'Write about that then. Write about that.'

Mr Yates walks on and I remove the cap from

my pen. I'm about to start writing when Eno lets off a massive guff. I wait for his civilisation-destroying trousers to excuse him, but . . .

. . . nothing happens.

He farts a second time – less of a guff this time and more of a quack.

A beat of silence.

And then laughter. A repetitive electronic *Ha!* coming from the area of Eno's bottom. It sounds more like the way a laugh is written than actually laughed. *Ha ha ha ha!*

'It's working,' says Malc. 'I think it's working.'

Eno looks around for the source of this laughter. It takes him a moment to realise it's coming from his own trousers. 'What's . . . wait . . . that's not right.'

And then his trousers make a robotic farting sound. It's more of a buzz than a bum trumpet – *Frrrrrrrttttt* – but it is music to my ears.

Malc laughs. Gloria laughs.

Eno's trousers laugh.

And then they fart and laugh and fart and laugh and fart and . . .

Eno is standing now and turning in small circles as he tries to get a good look at his own bum – he reminds me of Zem when he's chasing his tail or trying to clean himself.

And now everyone is laughing. Myself included. In fact, I'm laughing so hard it makes my eyes water. I'm laughing so much it makes my tummy hurt. The classroom is filled with laughter. And it seems that my classmates might just have a future after all.

My skin prickles, the laughter around me fades and I feel as if my insides are being squashed and rolled into a tiny ball. Everything fades to black and I'm gone.

32

HOW IT ENDS.
THE CHOCOLATE SHAKES ARE GOOD.
SOMETHING'S BEEN BOTHERING BOB.
A HEART-BEATY, STOMACH-CLENCHY,
FUZZY KIND OF FEELING.

This can't be how it ends . . .

I'm in my house again – or some future version of it.

Future Me and Future Gloria are here. But they don't look good.

Future Me lies on the floor, legs curled to his belly, arms flung wide. Glo is on the sofa, head tilted back, hair a mess, a line of drool at the corner of her mouth. Whatever hit them has hit them hard. There is no sign of baby Elvis.

And then Gloria groans, and uses the back of her hand to wipe the drool from her mouth.

'She's . . . she's still alive,' I say.

'They're sleeping,' says a quiet voice.

I look around but see no one.

'Si?'

'There is no Si,' says the voice. It's a friendly voice. 'I'm Martin.'

'Martin?'

'It stands for Modular Artificial Intelligence.'

'What's that?'

'Smart speaker, basically.'

'Why are they sleeping?' I say. 'What have you done to them?'

'Me?' says Martin. 'Nothing.'

Future Me stirs. His eyes flicker open, he yawns, stretches and pushes himself into a sitting position. 'Bob?' he says. 'When did you arrive?'

'Just. What's going on? Why are you sleeping?

Where's Si? What's with Martin? Where's Elvis?'

'Whoa,' says Future Me. 'One thing at a time.' He drags himself onto the sofa. 'Take a seat, you're making me nervous.'

'Can I get anyone anything?' asks Martin. 'Drink? Biscuit?'

'Coffee, please,' says Future Me.

'And for your guest?'

'The chocolate shakes are good,' says my future self.

'Do they have nanobots in them?'

He laughs. 'Just chocolate and ice cream.'

'In that case, yes. Please.'

Gloria opens one eye. ''Nother coffee please, Martin. Hey, Bob.'

We have our drinks in the kitchen. They were waiting on the kitchen counter when we got there. No robots, just a drinks machine hidden under the counter.

And the chocolate shake really is fantastic.

I'm nervous to ask, but the first question on my mind is: 'Elvis . . . is he OK?'

'He's teething,' says Gloria.

'And he's a terrible sleeper,' says Future Me. 'Keeps us up half the night.'

'But he's amazing,' says Glo.

'Where is he?'

'Malc took him to the swings.'

'Malc? Why? Aren't you allowed outside? Have they gone wild?'

Future Me laughs. 'I expect they're having a lot of fun. But everything's fine.'

'He took him out for an hour so we could catch up on a little sleep,' says Gloria.

'Sleep,' says Future Me, 'is the greatest gift you can give to a parent. Remember that.'

'Sorry,' I say. 'For disturbing you.'

'Don't be silly. We owe everything we have to you.'

'No super-intelligence?' I say.

'Never happened,' says Future Me. 'Although we think Martin is pretty super.'

'Thank you,' says Martin, and he sounds a little embarrassed.

Gloria asks: 'Would you like anything to eat at all?'

'Play music by The Beatles,' says Martin. 'Sure.'

'No,' says Future Me, and the impatient tone in his voice reminds me of Dad. 'I asked –'

'Actually,' I say, 'I quite like The Beatles.'

'Fine,' says Future Me, and Martin plays 'Yesterday'. It's not my favourite song, but it is kind of appropriate.

Gloria obviously gets it too. 'You did it,' she says, ruffling my hair. 'You saved the world, Bob.'

Future Me farts. 'More or less.'

'Do you still have farting flu?'

'Scientists created a vaccine a few years ago,' says Gloria. 'Now that there's no Si controlling us.'

'I ate some baby food at breakfast,' explains Future Me.

'Something's been bothering me,' I say.

And I'm not talking about the fact that my future self eats baby food for breakfast.

'If I stopped the egg landing in the volcano, why did we still get the farting flu in all those other futures?'

And then I fart.

Future Me laughs. 'I think you have your answer.'

I don't get it.

'When you first came here, you must have caught the farting flu from me or Glo.'

Gloria says, 'And then when you went back . . .'

'I took it with me?'

They both nod.

'So instead of stopping a pandemic, you caused one,' says Future Me.

I groan. 'That's one of those time-travel paradoxes, isn't it?'

'A sort of farty butterfly-effect type of thingy,' says Gloria.

'But you'll have the vaccine in a year or so,' says Future Me.

'A year!'

'The time will fly by,' says Future Me.

There is a sound in the hallway. The door opening and – a second later – closing.

A man's voice: 'Hello?'

'In the kitchen,' says Gloria.

A baby burbles.

'Elvis?' I ask.

Future Me nods. And I'm surprised at how excited I am to see my son.

'Hey, gang.' A large man walks into the kitchen. He has a baby strapped against his broad chest in a baby carrier.

'Hey, Malc,' says Gloria.

'Malcolm,' I say. 'It's you?'

'Have we met?' says the big man, taking a seat at the table.

'Malc,' says Future Me, 'meet . . . me.'

'You?'

'Past Me,' says Future Me. 'From when we were boys.'

'Time travel?' says Malc uncertainly.

'Remember that time with the midnight feast, the fart gloves, the flying ants and trapping Eno in the loos?' says Future Me.

'Course I remember,' says the Schnitz. 'You don't forget a thing like that.'

'Well,' I say, 'this is how all that ends.'

Malc looks nervous, confused and less than convinced.

'Milkshake?' says Future Me.

'Go on,' says Malc, instantly brightening. 'Strawberry, please.'

'Remember the milk and lemonade?' says Gloria.

'*Filk*,' say Malc and I at the same time.

There is a pause.

'It really is you,' says Malcolm.

'It's really me.'

'In that case,' says Malcolm, lifting Elvis from his harness, 'maybe you'd like to hold your son?'

He looks at Gloria, his eyes asking if this is OK, and Gloria nods, *yes*.

I take hold of baby Elvis and sit his bottom on the edge of the table so that we are more or less eye to eye.

'Hey, you,' I say.

Elvis tilts his head to one side as if trying to get a better look at me.

'Who's this?' says Future Me.

Elvis glances at Future Me, then turns his big bright eyes back to me. He holds my gaze for a second, then says:

'Dada?'

And I am filled with a warm, heart-beaty, stomach-clenchy, fuzzy kind of feeling. It might be love, I guess. But that sounds a bit embarrassing, doesn't it?

Whatever it is, it's weird and I can't handle much more of it.

'Take him,' I say quickly to my future self.

'Why, what's wrong?'

'Tingles,' I say. 'And they're coming on fast.'

Future Me lifts the baby into his arms and the tingles are already the drags.

Five more minutes would have been nice, but Time doesn't take requests.

'Till next time,' says Future Me.

Gloria gives my hair one final ruffle.

And it's bye-bye 2049.

WE CAN BE ANYTHING WE WANT.

I'm sitting at my desk again.

The entire class is laughing.

Eno's trousers laugh and fart and laugh.

Mr Yates glares at Eno, and while I feel a little bad for him, it feels good not to be the focus of the inspector's attention.

'Get those trousers off!' Mr Redrum says to Eno.

Eno looks confused for a moment and then begins undoing the button on the front of his trousers.

'Not *take them off*!' says Mr Redrum. '*Turn* them off. Now.'

'Oh,' says Eno. 'Right.' He shoves his hand down the front of his trousers, rummages around and gives something a firm tug. The pants fall silent.

'Thank goodness for that,' whispers Malc. 'I thought he was going to do himself a serious injury for a moment.'

'OK, everyone,' says Mr Redrum. 'Show's over. Let's get back to our work, shall we?'

One by one, my classmates lose interest in Eno, pick up their pens and carry on writing about what they want to be when they grow up, none of them (with the exception of Malcolm and Gloria) having any idea how close they came to a future spent connected to a giant fart tank.

I look down at my own workbook and the words: *When I grow up I want to be a dad.*

I cross out the word *dad*.

Not because I don't want to be one, but because I know that I will be, and now that the world is safe I don't need to worry about all that baby stuff for a good few years.

I glance at the Schnitz's workbook and see he's written *Secret Agent*.

And why not?

There are countless possible futures for all of us, and I'm sure that in one of them Agent Schnitzel is out there fighting baddies, defusing bombs and maybe even diving over the occasional volcano.

I pick up my pen and start again.

When I grow up I want to be . . . an explorer.

Truth is, I'm almost certainly destined to earn my wages being a history teacher. But that doesn't mean I can't do some exploring on the side. After all, I am a time traveller.

34

GHOSTS CAN'T SMELL.
BUT THEY CAN HUG.
TROUSERS OF DOOM.
ALMOST.

Walking home from school, me and Malc and Gloria share a cinnamon bun that Gloria found at the bottom of her bag. It's stale, but that just means it lasts longer.

Halfway home, I stop walking.

'I'm going to pop into the graveyard,' I say.

'Want us to come with you?' Gloria asks.

It would be nice to have some company, but I'm not sure my friends are ready to see my mum as a ghost just yet. And more importantly, I don't think my mum will appear if there are other people around.

I shake my head. 'I'll be fine.'

'Band practice tomorrow?' says Malc.

I flash him a rock salute. 'Definitely.'

'I'll bring my tambourine,' says Gloria.

Malc and I groan. And then all three of us laugh.

I say goodbye to my friends and make my way to the graveyard.

It's a bright evening and the sun is shining directly onto the bench closest to Mum's grave. That's where I'm sitting, with my eyes closed, enjoying the warmth on my face when the voice speaks.

'What happened to your uniform?'

And I know it's Mum before I see her.

I open my eyes, turn my head and she's sitting right there beside me. 'Been saving the world,' I tell her. 'Again.'

'Hug,' says Mum, opening her arms wide.

'I'm kind of icky and stinky.'

'I'm a ghost,' Mum says. 'Can't smell a thing.'

She feels real, though, and the hug is a good one. Even with her baby bump between us.

'Where have you been?' I ask her.

Mum's eyes flick quickly towards her grave and then away. 'Nowhere,' she says. 'The question is, where have *you* been?'

'2049.'

'Wow. Big jump. You'd have been, what . . . thirty-seven? What was happening?'

'Farting flu, flying robots, fart fuel.'

Mum laughs. 'I meant with *you*. What's happening with you in the future?'

'I kind of married Gloria,' I say, blushing.

Mum laughs. 'You and Gloria! Yes, I can see how that might happen.'

'I can't,' I say. 'But it did. Or does.'

'Well, don't let your dad get too drunk on the big day,' Mum says. 'He always gets carried away at weddings.' She laughs. 'Come to think of it, he got quite tipsy at our wedding. Danced on a table.'

'You're kidding?'

She shakes her head. 'There was a candle on the table and your dad's trouser leg caught fire mid-pirouette. He could have gone up in flames if your granddad hadn't thrown a jug of water at him.'

Candles and trousers, I think. *Sounds a lot like my own day.*

'Trousers of doom,' I say.

'What's that?' says Mum.

I'm just about to explain, but before I get the chance she winces.

'Did the baby kick?'

The baby, in this case, being me.

Mum nods. 'I think you're' – she rubs her tummy – 'looks like you're getting the tingles.'

Which means any minute now she will be gone.

'But you've only just got here,' I say.

'That's the trouble with time travel,' says Mum. 'It's almost impossible to control.'

'*Almost?*'

Mum waggles her hand this way and that. 'There are a few – ouch.' She clutches at her tummy and lets out a small gasp.

'What do you mean, "almost"?'

'I'm sorry, sweetheart –' she leans in and hugs me again – 'I have to g . . .'

But before she can finish the sentence, Mum fades to nothing in my arms.

Almost, I think.

What did she mean by almost?

35

A JOB FOR BOB.
A PLAN FOR FATHER'S DAY.
CHEESE-AND-SARDINE PIZZA.

Dad was on a work call when I got home so I changed out of my smelly school uniform, hid it in the laundry basket and went down to the garage. Which is a lot nicer now that the cobwebs have gone.

I've just about finished cleaning the Machine of Ultimate Velocity when Dad pops his head around the door.

'Hello,' he says. 'You're home late. Didn't get detention again, did you?'

'Not this time.'

But I did save the world.

'I'm impressed,' he says, as if he's read my mind.

'Why?'

He point at the MOUV. 'You, cleaning your bike. What's that all about?'

'I got a job.'

Dad stares at me for a count of one, two, three. 'A what?'

'I got a paper round. Stopped off at Mr Miles's newsagents on the way home from school.'

Dad's smile is so big and simple it makes me laugh. 'When do you start?'

'Six thirty tomorrow morning.'

'Bob,' he says, coming over and kissing the top of my head. 'I'm proud of you, son.'

Mr Miles is going to pay me fifteen pounds a week for three morning deliveries, plus a bag of sweets and a can of pop on a Friday.

Also – and I know this sounds mushy – the look on

Dad's face, the way it makes me feel when Dad says he's proud of me – that's worth a whole lot more.

'What you going to spend it on?' Dad says.

'Dunno,' I tell him.

But this isn't true.

When I explained about needing the money for Father's Day, Mr Miles offered to give me my first week's wages in advance. And I know exactly what I'm going to get with it.

Sausages. And bacon and eggs and beans and toast. And I'm going to serve it to him in bed. Sleep, Future Me said, is the greatest gift you can give to a parent. So this Father's Day, I'm going to give Dad a long lie-in followed by a massive breakfast. Maybe I'll cook one for me too.

And if there's any money left over, I'm going to get a new felt pen so I can continue colouring in my trousers after they've been through the wash.

'How about we celebrate your new job with pizza?'

Dad says. 'A load of cheese and sardines arrived this morning – we'll use those.'

I doubt sardines have ever been used as a pizza topping before. And after tonight I doubt they'll be used again. But do you know what? I really don't care.

'Sounds amazing,' I say.

'And afterwards, maybe I'll make some popcorn and we can watch a movie.'

'A movie sounds great,' I say. 'But I might skip the popcorn.'

'Strange boy,' says Dad. 'Right, I'll get cooking while you finish off in here. Oh, and – he wrinkles his nose – 'take a shower, would you?'

I laugh. 'Definitely.'

'And Bob?'

'Yes?'

'Take your time.'

Dad winks as he says this, and heads inside to make supper.

We hope you loved your Piccadilly Press book!

For all the latest bookish news, freebies and exclusive content, sign up to the Piccadilly Press newsletter – scan the QR code or visit lnk.to/PiccadillyNewsletter

Follow us on social media:

bonnierbooks.co.uk/PiccadillyPress